CHALLENGES

Jean Reddy

CHALLENGES

Jean Reddy

CONTENTS

DEDICATION

To my beloved children, who are so infinitely precious to me, each of them individual and special:- Mary, Alan, Susan and Sally.

May your lives be blessed with love and happiness.

With all my love
Mum

JR

This is a story based on true life. The names of the characters have been changed to protect the individuals.

CHAPTER 1

1951

Margaret thought back to when she had left school at 15 years of age and her only qualifications had been her secretarial skills. She was good at speed typing, her Pitman shorthand was quite good and her mathematics were excellent. The Careers Officer had advised her that there were good jobs available locally and had been sure she could place her satisfactorily. Her first job had been as a clerical officer within the wages department at a local factory. The money was not good but it was a start. Her mother had been pleased and said her salary would help a great deal, instructing her to bring home her wages envelope unopened. She had been given a small allowance and her bus fares to work. The job was pretty menial, but she had learnt to use a comptometer which had fascinated her. This meant that she had had to learn decimalisation, as the machine only worked sums out for you with that method.

A couple of evenings a week she went with her friends Janet and Josie to the local dance hall, where they enjoyed the music and often danced with the young men before going to the local café for a coffee or an ice cream. One evening she had danced with a young man called Sandy. He had been very jolly and teased her a lot. He was nice looking, and had sandy coloured hair. He had asked if he could take her home as he had a car, and she had accepted. Wow, what a car, a little MG sports, her friends had watched her climb in and tie a scarf round her hair. It had felt grand. Sandy was very nice and she had been taken everywhere by him. First to the cinema, where they had sat in the circle, and he had given her a lovely box of chocolates, and then he had taken her home to meet his mother who lived in a luxury service flat in Richmond. One weekend he had taken her down into the country and explained to her that his parents actually lived in Sussex, where they owned a big estate. Her eyes had popped out of her head when they drove up the drive leading to an enormous house. Sandy introduced her to his father, and gave her coat to the maid who had been standing quietly in the background. After taking afternoon tea, which had consisted of tiny sandwiches and cakes all nicely set out on silver stands, and the most delicate cup and saucer had been placed in her hands. Sandy had taken her to the stables. She had loved the horses, but had been a little afraid of them as they were so big. Her mother liked Sandy, he had always arrived with a gift for her, sometimes a box of chocolates, sometimes a bunch of flowers. She had been delighted, and had loved the fact that he had the lovely MG sports car.

She had been at the firm for three weeks when she was asked to go down into the factory and collect the clock cards. As she walked through the factory there had been lots of wolf calls from the men working at the various machines. It had been very embarrassing, and she had quickly collected the cards from the clock machine and was just making a hasty retreat when a young man had stepped forward and opened the connecting door into the office building for her. She had thanked him and hurried back to her office. Gary often appeared from nowhere on the days she had to collect the cards, and a few weeks later had invited her to the cinema with him. He had seemed nice enough, so she had accepted.

Gary had taken her on the bus to the cinema, and stopped off at the local sweet shop and bought a bag of toffees. When they arrived at the cinema he had bought two tickets for the front of the stalls, commonly known as the 'pits'. They were the cheapest seats and you had to look up at the screen, stretching your neck. They had seen the film 'Belles on their Toes'. Gary had moaned that he had to get her back home before 10.30pm, missing the last part of the picture, but her mother had insisted. She had known her mother did not like Gary. She had always let Sandy bring her home a little later.

Sandy had become jealous of Gary and it had not been long before Sandy had started taking other girls home from the dance hall. Janet and Josie insisted she go with them to the Hammersmith Palais one Saturday night. It had been fun dancing to the Ted Heath band and listening to the resident singer Dennis Lotis. Josie was mesmerised by him and was on cloud nine when he came down off the stage and danced with her. The girls started to go regularly each Saturday evening, it was great fun, but the only time she could see Gary was a Saturday evening. He worked late most evenings during the week, and his only free time was Saturday. Gradually her visits to the Hammersmith Palais became fewer and fewer.

Gary had taken her home to meet his mother and some of his brothers. He had six brothers, though only three lived at home. The older ones were married with families. His mother lived in one of the council houses about a mile from her own mother's house. Mrs Pearce was a very nice homely lady, and cooked very nice apple pies. It was nice to see that Gary's mother doted on him as well as on his brothers. She was a widow, her husband having died from tuberculosis a few years before. Gradually over the weeks she had seen more of Gary than of Sandy, and she felt sorry for Gary because he had very little money. They often went for walks across the common and into Richmond Park, or strolled along the river bank of the Thames towards Richmond. They would walk hand in hand, and often Gary would put his arm round her, telling her how much he cared

3

about her. This had been music to her ears. She had never felt loved in her life, except by John her brother.

After a few months she had decided to change jobs. She wanted to earn some more money and do a job which she would enjoy, as well as the fact that she did not like the office atmosphere, with the other girls chiding her about Gary all the time. So she had gone to work in a fishmongers as a cashier. Although she had learnt a lot about fish, she did not like having to continually bath because she smelt of it, so that job had not lasted long. She had tried various jobs, but she knew for certain she wanted to work with and for people. However thanks to her mother she had no qualifications. What was she to do? She tried another office job at a wholesalers; she quite liked the people she worked with, and they did not chide her about her private life so she had stayed. The money was better and she had over £1 to herself each week, so that she could buy herself a coat which she badly needed. She had seen the coat in a shop window for £4, a light brown swagger coat which had suited her. She had put £1 down and gradually paid the balance over a few weeks before she could have it, but it had been worth it. The new coat was terrific, and it kept her lovely and warm on cold days. When she had left school it had been early September and now there were cold March winds. She had been cold all winter.

She had slipped into a routine, going to work, then helping her mother at home, and on Saturday nights going out with Gary. Her two friends continued to encourage her to go with them to the dance halls but she knew that Gary did not like it if she went, and he himself did not like dancing. He did not like classical music very much either, and her own interest in the piano started to wane. Her mother commented that she rarely practised, and that when she played there were a lot of mistakes in her playing.

4

She had continued to see Gary, much against her mother's wishes, and her relationship with her mother, never very good, became much worse. There were times she hated going home. Life had remained very much the same over the next two years, though she had seen less of her friends, and was seeing Gary more often. She decided to try and improve her relationship with her mother. One day as she was leaving work, she passed a florist shop and saw some violets at the front of the shop window. She thought they looked lovely and felt her mother would love them. She went inside and bought a bunch, while the assistant wrapped them in some pretty paper. She took them home with her on the bus, humming to herself. She was sure her mother would love the flowers. She walked up the garden path and into the kitchen where her mother was preparing the evening meal. She handed the flowers to her mother, who looked at them, and then asked, 'Is this a sprat to catch a mackerel?' Margaret was unsure what she meant. 'I thought you would like them Mum,' she said. 'I bought them especially for you.'

Mrs Trent ungraciously took the flowers from Margaret and put them down near the sink, and then got on with the dinner. She had not thanked Margaret for them, nor commented about them during the whole of the evening. Margaret had felt devastated. The flowers had remained near the sink, her mother had not even put them in a vase. Margaret was upset. The flowers had cost so little, only 9d, but she thought that her mother would at least say thank you. There appeared to be no way she could bridge the gap between her mother and herself.

She often sat with Gary in her house in the evenings when her mother was working at the local pub. They would sit on the settee and cuddle. Gary told her that when he became eighteen in October he would be conscripted into the Army, and she had dreaded the thought that he would be leaving her. One night she had clung to him, and pleaded with him not to go, but he had told her he had to or they would arrest him. How she had cried, Gary had consoled her, and told her he loved her. He had kissed her deeply, and then pulled her tightly into his arms. She had known nothing about sex, but she knew she wanted him to make love to her. She could feel his body close to hers, and was quite positive she needed him. After all he loved her and she loved him. Her heart had ruled her head, she needed to be loved, and here was Gary so close, so warm and comforting. His hands moved over her body, and she gave herself to him.

Later that evening she had lain next to him, listening to his promises. They would get engaged. She had been ecstatic. They would get married. Her heart had leapt with joy. She would be able to leave home and live with him, somewhere away from her mother.

CHAPTER 2

A few weeks later Gary had received his call-up papers, and she was not looking forward to his leaving for Catterick Camp in North Yorkshire where he was to undergo six weeks training in the Royal Signals.

Gary had told her he would speak to her mother, but it was some weeks before he plucked up the courage to call on her. He had known it would not be easy, and that Mrs Trent did not like him very much. He did not understand this - he had a fairly good job, albeit the money was not much - but they would manage. The firm would hold his job open for him after he had completed his two years. While he was in the army he was assured that a married quarter and a reasonable pay would be given him.

Unfortunately Mrs Trent became very angry when he approached her, and told him in no uncertain terms that she would never let her daughter marry him, and told him to go back to the council estate where he belonged. Gary had relayed the conversation back to Margaret, who was devastated. Her horrible mother did not want her to be happy, ever. She had cried bitter tears of frustration. They could not marry, without Mrs Trent's agreement, as she was still under twenty one. She had told her friend Janet all about it, who said, the only way would be to take Mrs Trent to court. What a wonderful idea! Not letting the grass grow under her feet she had taken the bus into town and made an application at the court house.

In October Gary had left for Catterick. She had gone with him on that fateful day up to Kings Cross Station in London, where he was to catch the big steam train to Yorkshire. Gary had been very nervous about leaving home and going to Yorkshire. Margaret was not feeling all that well and was terribly upset that he was going so far away, for so long. She tried not to cry, but she was so choked up inside that she was beside herself. They rode together on the Underground from Richmond to Kings Cross, and then searched for the right platform for his train. There were so many trains going to so many places. It reminded Margaret of when she started her journey to Wales, when she had been evacuated during the war. Now Gary was going away and he would be so lonely, just like she had been. She clung to him, sobbing. 'I don't want you to go,' she kept saying. The whistle blew and he climbed aboard the train, leaning out of the carriage window, assuring her he would return soon. Life was horrible, she had watched his train pull out of the station, and felt desolate. Margaret was openly crying as she retraced her steps to Richmond, not caring that people were staring at the tears flowing down her face. What an awful day.

******

When the notice had been served on her mother, Mrs Trent had been very angry, and some four weeks later she was beside herself when the court gave permission for the marriage. Margaret had been proud of Gary standing in the witness box giving evidence, he looked so smart in his army uniform. After the hearing he returned to Catterick. He wrote back explaining that he now had to get permission from his commanding officer.

A week went by before he wrote and told her that he had been granted a 72 hour pass to get married, she could now name the day. What joy!

The wedding had taken place at the local church, and with her friends Janet and Josie as her bridesmaids Margaret had married Gary. It had been a lovely sunny day, but she had not noticed as she was so busy with all the arrangements. Her mother stayed in the kitchen at the house;

they were still not speaking. Her brother John and his wife Elsa arrived and also her Aunt Daisy. Upstairs in her small bedroom hung the wedding dress she had chosen. It was made of satin and tulle and had a tight bodice and a flowing skirt, which made her feel grand, and a little bolero of white lace to match the dress. She had chosen a short circular veil held in place by a little wire-tiara. The whole ensemble had cost her £7 10s but was all she had been able to afford. The dress had been on a model in the window of a bridal shop in Hammersmith which she had seen when she last went to the Palais. When she had tried it on in the shop it had fitted perfectly, but on the morning of the wedding she had difficulty doing up the zip. Gosh it did feel tight!

Janet and Josie had very similar dresses in pale blue with coronets of blue flowers. Unfortunately things started to go wrong an hour before the wedding. Firstly her mother decided she would attend the wedding. Then the boy from the flower shop arrived on his bike, and on checking found he had all the buttonhole flowers for Gary's family that should have been delivered to the groom's house. The boy promised he would cycle there with the buttonholes.

Half an hour before the wedding, four wedding cars arrived. Two came from one firm, and two from another. She had enquired the price from both firms but had only booked the cars with one. Goodness, what was she to do? John took charge and sorted it out. Even so, one car should have collected Gary and his brother Sid who was the best man. Margaret was beside herself, it was all going wrong. John calmed her down, and they set off together in the big old Packard car bedecked with white ribbon.

The wedding itself went well, and things started to improve. The 'reception' was being held at Gary's home, though her mother stated categorically she would not go to 'that house.' Early that morning everyone had lent a hand making sandwiches and Mrs Pearce had made some sausage rolls, as well as a little cake. Unbeknown to them one of Gary's brothers had decided to play a prank on him, and had spiked his drink. Gary was not used to drinking so it had not taken much to make him merry. All of a sudden he had toppled over and lay prone on the floor. Two of his brothers had carried him upstairs. This did not bode well, the car was waiting to take them to her sister May's house in London, where they were going to stay for a while, but the driver was not happy about taking him in the car in a drunken state. Eventually after much discussion they set out. The driver had Gary up in the front seat, the other side of the glass petition.

This was not how it was meant to be. Where was all the romantic going away bit? She had visualised him with an arm around her in the back seat. She was so unhappy. As well as that he was still drunk.

When they arrived in London her brother-in-law made Gary drink lots of coffee, and walked him up and down the road while she sat and cried. Eventually he was put to bed, and she climbed in beside him. It was a fold-me-down bed just four feet wide which creaked and groaned every time she moved. No wedding night for her. Gary fell fast asleep.

To make up for this Gary took her for a day out at Southend-on-Sea. He wanted to go on all the rides at the fun fair, which just made her feel very sick. He bought her some jellied eels which made her feel even more nauseous. There was only one more day to go before he had to return to Yorkshire. Not feeling well did not help, but she once again experienced the feelings of loss coming on. He reminded her that there was only a very short time left before he would be posted, and hopefully they would be given a married quarter somewhere in the south. This appeased her a little, and she put up a brave front when he once again caught the train up north.

She continued to live at her sister's house, but decided to pass the time getting a job. Within a few days she started work at Yardleys cosmetic company as an export typist. It paid good money and was soon into a routine. She had been sick some mornings and thought she had flu. Her sister told her to go to see the doctor.

He was a kindly man, who examined her. She sat in front of his desk wondering what was wrong with her, and if she would lose her job if she had to take time off. The doctor sat down, smiled at her and said, 'Well Mrs Pearce I am pleased to tell you, you are pregnant.' She stared at him in total disbelief. Somehow she left the surgery and made her way to a little café and ordered a cup of tea. Pregnant. Oh dear what would happen now? The doctor had assured her she could continue work for a further three months. Well she would be moving soon, and Gary would look after her, she would be an army wife. She caught the bus back to her sister's house and wrote a long letter to her husband. She was sure he would be pleased.

A few days later back came a letter. She tore it open and started to read. She read it two or three times. Gary was not pleased, he pointed out they had no money and nowhere to live. The army could not allocate them a married quarter, and he was being relocated to Bulford Camp in Wiltshire. There was no available accommodation for them there. What would happen to her? She could not continue to stay in her sister's overcrowded house. May had only agreed to provide a temporary solution for them. She ran upstairs to her bedroom and threw herself on the bed and cried, eventually falling asleep. She awoke with a start a few hours later. It all came back to her. What should she tell her sister? She decided to say nothing. The following week Gary was posted to Bulford. After only a few days he wrote to her again telling her he had found some accommodation just outside the camp where they could both stay. He had obtained permission to live out of camp, and he would be paid an allowance for his rent. Thank goodness! She excitedly told May she was moving out and going to live in a bungalow, sharing with an elderly couple in Amesbury, just two miles from Bulford. She would be with Gary. How wonderful.

CHAPTER 3

The bungalow was rather old, and to her disappointment they only had one room. The double bed took up a large part of the room. In the corner stood a small old table on which sat an electric ring. This was to be her cooker. Mrs Caplin showed her around, the bathroom was on the other side of the bungalow, and she was told that there was only cold water, except on Sundays when the range in the kitchen was lit by her husband, when there was hot water all day. The kitchen range was also available to cook anything in on Sundays as well. The large garden was quite wild and unkept. Mrs Caplin explained that her husband worked all week and on Sundays liked to rest, but sometimes he went out with a scythe to cut it down a bit.

Gary seemed to think the arrangement was fine, and Margaret hid her feelings. At least they would be together. Everything looked reasonable when the sun shone, but they were now in winter and the days were darker and it rained a lot. Everything seemed dismal. The bed was old and creaked, and it was very squeezy to sit at the table. The one saving grace was Wilma, short for Wilhemena. A black and white, rough coated mongrel dog. They fell in love with each other instantly. The dog jumped up and licked her, her tongue never stopping. Margaret stroked the dog and from that day they were the best of pals and gave her someone to confide in. When Wilma had a problem, such as a tick in her paws, Margaret would remove it gently for her. When Margaret felt unloved and miserable, Wilma would listen and lick her, as if to say, I understand, but I love you.

As her body grew in size, it became more difficult for her to get about. Christmas came and went. She was busy knitting little matinee coats and bootees, and was about to start making a shawl. She had lots of time on her hands, and Gary was away at the camp nearly every day for long hours. Mrs Caplin often went out to play bridge with her friends, so the days sometimes dragged. Gary only seemed to want her for sex, as he often remarked, now she was pregnant they did not have to be careful any more and it was a great opportunity to have sex. As the weeks progressed Margaret started to dread it, notwithstanding it was uncomfortable. She wanted Gary to put his arms round her and assure her he loved her, but when she chided him about it, he only said, 'I'm here aren't I?'

She learnt that she was to have the baby at Tidworth Military Hospital, some eight miles away. She went on the bus to the hospital to register and for an antenatal appointment. All was well. The baby was due at the beginning of April. She was scared about the birth, and had no idea how the baby would be born. No one had told her. These fears she kept to herself.

The village of Amesbury was just down the hill from where she lived. It was a lovely village, with a Post Office and a few little shops and a garage, where people filled up with petrol, or took their cars to be serviced. The grocers shop sold most of things she needed, and she was able to buy small quantities such as two rashers of bacon for Sunday breakfast, and just three eggs, which had to last the week. Gary only brought home a small amount of money, and after paying the rent to Mrs Caplin it meant she had to be very careful indeed on what she purchased. She had been given milk tokens at the hospital, so that was one thing she did not have to buy.

Margaret often walked down the hill into the village, and took Wilma for a walk on the lead. Wilma was great company, and would sit outside the shops patiently for her.

At the beginning of March she started having severe backache, and Mrs Caplin told her that it would not be long before the baby was born. This gripped her with fear. The unknown. The backache became worse over the next week, and she started to feel sick. Mrs Caplin insisted one night on calling an ambulance for her, as she lay in agony on the creaking bed. Gary arrived home about 9pm just as the ambulance arrived, and went with her to the hospital. The journey was painful, the army ambulance had primitive springing, and the country lanes were not smooth. But she got there, and after being examined was told that these were not labour pains, she had a kidney infection, and would have to stay in the hospital, probably until the baby was born. She was on the antenatal ward, and other women were admitted and then proceeded to have their babies, and move to the postnatal ward. But not she. She had to stay put and drink pints of water and take huge capsules to clear the infection. Even when she was better, she went no further than the end of the ward.

The nursing sisters were Irish and very humorous, she quite liked them. It was from them she learnt how the baby was to born. However, she was not prepared for how painful it would be. Three weeks later she knew. Oh how she knew. Surely there was something wrong, it was unendurable. She cried. Again she was on her own. They put her into a side ward so as not to disturb the other women. The pain enveloped her. It went on all day and well into the night. At 1 o'clock they took her along the corridor to the labour ward, and showed her the gas and air machine. In just two minutes she had learnt the technique, out of pure necessity. A whole hour went by, the pain excruciating, until the moment when she felt the urge to push, and very slowly her beautiful baby girl was born. The pain just disappeared, all she could think of was how beautiful she was, a tiny pink bundle, she looked so sweet. They let her hold her for a few minutes before whisking her off to the nursery. Margaret glowed, she had a baby girl.

She was moved to the postnatal ward, and a well deserved sleep, only to be woken some three hours later to feed the baby. She was so tired, but also elated. All the babies were laid out on a large trolley rolled up in white cotton blankets. She was handed her baby and shown how to put the baby to her breast to feed her. It took a while but Margaret soon got the hang of it. The baby was then taken back to the nursery.

Husbands were allowed to visit once a day between 7pm and 8pm, so many hours elapsed before Gary arrived. He came into the ward smiling, pecked her on the cheek, and said 'Well done,' then went on to ask 'What are we going to call her? I was expecting a boy, so I have not thought of a name for a girl. I know, we will call her after my mother - Maud' he said.

Margaret looked at him in astonishment. 'Oh no, we need a nice name for her, what about Anne?' They argued about the name of the baby for most of the visit, but eventually he agreed to Anne. Thank goodness, she thought, I could never call a baby Maud!

After twelve days she was allowed out of hospital. Having been protected from the cold weather inside the hospital, she was unprepared for the weather outside. It had been snowing heavily and she was frightened she would slip carrying the baby, who was snugly wrapped in the shawl she had made. They walked through the hedgerows to the bus stop, and waited for what seemed an age for the bus. Eventually it arrived and they were transported back to Amesbury.

Mr and Mrs Caplin were quite excited, and asked to hold the baby. Anne was a very good baby and rarely cried, but Margaret soon learned that Mrs Caplin could not stand to hear a baby cry, and so she had to purchase a dummy in the village shortly after her return home. Mr Caplin scythed the grass under the clothes line so that she could do the washing including all the nappies every day. In the winter with the weather being rather inclement some days were difficult in getting things dry. Gary decided to spend a few pounds on a secondhand Tilley lamp which served two purposes. Firstly to keep the room warm for the baby, and secondly to dry the washing especially the nappies.

With the Government grant they purchased a pram, which doubled as a cot, as there was no room for both, (nor was there enough money for both). And so they managed for a few months. Her mother was delighted with the birth of yet another grandchild and invited them all up to Richmond. Gary acquired a weekend pass, and they went up on the Royal Blue Coach, direct to Richmond. As soon as they arrived Mrs Trent took the baby from Margaret. There were no real words of greeting to either Gary or herself. If she hadn't been breastfeeding the baby, she would never have held her. Her mother was besotted with the baby, a relationship that was to last until her mother died many years later. Anne could have anything. Her mother bought the baby clothes and toys, a baby bath, and some really soft muslin nappies. The weekend soon passed, and life returned to normal.

Gary could not wait for her postnatal examination, after which their sexual activities began once more. Margaret was scared she would become pregnant again and talked to the doctor at the hospital about this.

He had her fitted with a cap and said that this would be all right. She hoped so. Gary pestered her all the time.

CHAPTER 4

It was not that she did not love Gary, she did, but he never made her feel loved. Although she knew he loved the baby, he was also jealous of Anne taking up so much of her time. She knew her feelings for Gary had changed in some way, but decided not to analyse it. What with the baby, and the affection she received from Wilma she was fairly happy. Wilma followed her everywhere, and would sit by the pram when Anne was asleep and 'guard her'.

The months passed and spring changed to summer. It was lovely in the country with warm balmy days. She fell into a regular routine, until one day in August she came home to find Gary at the bungalow in the middle of the afternoon. 'Hello,' she said, 'What are you doing here so early?'

He looked frightened. He kept peering out of the window. 'What's up Gary?' she repeated.

'The redcaps are after me,' he said.

She was amazed, 'What for?' she asked.

He explained that he had been helping a mate out, so he thought, who had asked him to move a lorry.

'But Gary you can't drive, and you have no licence,' she said.

'I know, but I can ride a motorbike and I thought it would be much the same,' he replied. He looked out of the window again. 'I backed the lorry into the cookhouse wall, and there is a lot of damage. I ran away so that I could tell you what is happening. They will put me in the guard house until I am court martialled.' At that moment a jeep turned into the driveway, with two military police on board.

'I have to go Margaret, I will try and let you know if I am sent to Colchester Glass House. Unfortunately if I am sent there my pay will stop. I am sorry.'

She stood there staring at him. Wilma barked at the policemen, and the next minute they were escorting Gary down the front path to the jeep. The noise woke Anne, and Margaret simply froze. The tears flowed down her cheeks unchecked. Gary was gone. What was she to do?

It took some while for her to digest the situation. Outside the sunny day had turned dark, and clouds covered the sky. That night she could not sleep, not only worrying about the situation but also as a thunderstorm raged overhead. There were loud clashes of thunder and sharp streaks of lightning. It was raining hard, and by early morning she had made up her mind, she would have to go to the camp and talk to the Commanding Officer. Once she had made up her mind, nothing would shake her. She knew it was still raining hard, but Anne would be fine in her pram.

At 8 o'clock, she set off squelching along the lane, and out onto the main road leading to the camp. Her coat was soaked, as well as her headscarf. It was two miles on foot, but there was no other way. Her worries urged her on.

She arrived at the guard house just before 9am, parked the pram and went inside and spoke to the sergeant on duty. 'I want to see the Commanding Officer, please,' she said. He looked her up and down. 'Have you an appointment Madam?' he asked.

'No I haven't but I must see him urgently,' she replied. He disappeared through a door and was gone for some time.

He emerged some ten minutes later and told her that Captain Cooper would see her now. He ushered her through the door, and into a small room where an officer sat behind a desk.

'Good morning Mrs Pearce,' he said as he rose and put out his hand. 'How can I help you?'

She burst into tears. 'It's about my husband, Gary,' she cried. 'He is going to be locked up and I don't know when I will see him again.'

He asked her to sit down and ordered the young soldier just behind her to bring in a cup of tea. 'Mrs Pearce will you tell me all about it. I know he is here in the guard house, but as yet nothing has happened, and the matter is yet to be dealt with.'

She told him all she knew, including the long walk this morning with Anne.

'Where is the baby?' he asked.

'She is outside in her pram.'

He had listened quietly. Suddenly he got up and gave orders for the baby to be brought into the guard house, pram and all. A young solider brought in a steaming mug of tea which she was really grateful for. Her clothes were soaking wet. Captain Cooper noticed this and suggested she take off her coat and scarf, and despatched an orderly to put them near the stove in the main guard room to dry. She sipped the hot tea slowly, cupping the mug with her cold wet hands. The officer walked over to a chart on the wall.

The Captain came and sat back behind his desk, he appeared deep in thought. 'This is a serious situation, I have just seen the order on the wall, and it would appear that Private Pearce jumped into a 3 ton lorry, without permission, started it up and backed it into the cookhouse wall, the damage will cost a lot of money to repair. It would go into hundreds.' He sat staring ahead of him for some while. 'Mrs Pearce, I think the best way forward would be for you to see Private Pearce on your own and suggest to him that it would be in his better interest to admit the deed, and when I ask him if he wants to be tried by me or sent for court martial, he requests I deal with the mater. I can only say I will do my best, knowing that it would be you and the

21

baby that suffers the most from this dilemma. What do you say?'

Margaret replied nervously. 'I will talk to Gary and make the suggestion. I am sure he would be grateful for your help, Captain, I know I am. Goodness knows how long he would be at the Glasshouse if he were found guilty, and if he did not receive any pay how would we live? I'll talk to him.'

She was shown into a small room with a large wooden table in the centre and a chair either side of it. She was still shaking but the tea had warmed her a little. The door on the far side opened and Gary was brought in. He was amazed to see her, and kept apologising to her, continually saying he was sorry. She told him what the Captain had suggested, and he readily agreed he would ask for him to deal with the matter, when he was brought before him later that morning. Her eyes were filled with unshed tears. The five minutes was soon up.

Gary was taken back through the door at the far end of the room and she was once more sat alone. She could hear Anne crying, it was nearly time for her feed. Standing up, she moved towards the door behind her and went back along the corridor to the Captain's room. Having told him what had transpired, Captain Cooper called out to one of the soldiers. 'Private Williams please bring my jeep round to the front of the guard room, and arrange to take Mrs Pearce and the baby home to Amesbury.' The soldier saluted, turned on his heel and disappeared.

'Don't worry too much my dear, things look black at the moment, but I will be as lenient as I am able to, however, he will have to be punished.' She nodded, and with that he extended his hand, and shook hers while opening the door for her to precede him back into the main guardroom where Anne was the centre of attention. Minutes later she was on her way back to the bungalow, with the pram in the back of the jeep and Anne safely on her lap. What a morning!

CHAPTER 5

Late that afternoon an army motorcyclist rode up the drive. He parked the vehicle and came up the front steps and knocked on the door. Margaret answered the door. He handed her a letter and told her it was from Captain Cooper.

As he departed, she tore open the envelope. A single sheet of paper advised her that Gary, who had pleaded guilty to the offence, had been given 14 days CB (confined to barracks) and was to lose 2s 6d a week from his pay for a year. While on CB he would do extra guard duty, and would have to report to the guard room every four hours. He would return to Amesbury in 15 days time. The letter was signed, best wishes, Captain Cooper.

What a relief, and what a nice man was the Captain. She smiled for the first time that day. They were not to lose Gary's pay and he would be home in two weeks time. She hoped Gary appreciated what she had done. The rain had stopped and the afternoon suddenly appeared brighter.

She settled down to wait, and to look after Anne. She spent time spring cleaning the room and making a long christening dress for Anne. She was determined the baby would be baptised as soon as possible. As there was no money to buy material, she found one of her white silk nightdresses and cut the tiny garment out of it, stitching it all by hand, as she had no sewing machine.

The two weeks flew by, and suddenly Gary was back. She ran down the drive to meet him, and flew into his arms. He kissed her and held her tight. They stayed locked in an embrace for some time, with Wilma running and jumping and barking too. All the commotion awoke Anne. Gary bent and picked up the baby from the pram and held her. It was a good day, and that evening while they lay side by side in their creaky bed after Gary had made love to her, she told him of her plans for the christening. They would go back to Richmond so that the family members could attend. She wanted her brother John and his wife Elsa to be godparents.

He was allowed a weekend pass for the end of July. Anne would be nearly four months old then. It seemed perfect. The dress was finished. She had edged it all with lace and embroidered tiny daisies over the bottom of the long skirt. A little bonnet completed the outfit. It was fit for a princess.

She had written to her mother, and told her they would be coming up and asked to stay two nights at the house. She wrote to Janet and asked her to book the church. It turned out to be a very nice day and everyone seemed happy. The sun shone and Anne looked resplendent in her lovely christening gown and bonnet. John and his wife seemed very proud to becoming Anne's godparents. Even Mrs Trent seemed in an extremely good mood, although she liked to hold Anne most of the time, and was reluctant to part with her for the actual baptism. But on the whole it was a good day and Margaret was pleased.

Mrs Trent wanted to know what Gary was going to do when he left the army the following year. He told her his old job had been kept open for him, and he hoped to get a small rise in wages, now that he was a married man. You could tell she was not impressed, and then asked where they would live. He replied they had not thought about that as yet. They were amazed when she said, 'Well you can come and live here for a short while until you find a flat.'

Later when they were on their own Gary said, 'I don't want to live in the same house as your mother. She does not like me.'

'Well it will be a start love,' Margaret had replied.

'I do not want to live here, don't you understand?' He shouted at her.

'I know mother does not get on well with you, but it will get better, I am sure it will,' she cried.

Gary would have none of it, and stormed out.

They returned back to Amesbury on the Royal Blue coach. It was very late, but Gary had to be back in barracks the following morning. He hardly spoke to her, and every time she tried to make conversation he pretended not to hear. She could tell he was sulking. There were times when he seemed very childish.

The months flew by. Anne started sitting up in her pram. It was getting too small for her to sleep in at night. However, they had no money to buy a cot, nor was there room to put one up. Gary's eldest brother Jim offered them a secondhand cot, but it had to be transported from Wincanton some 25 miles away. Margaret talked to Mrs Caplin about the problem. She suggested that they put the cot up in the small spare room. This seemed a marvellous solution. So Jim borrowed an old van and brought it up to Amesbury.

Another Christmas came and went. They had to stay in Wiltshire, as Gary was on guard duty for the whole week before Christmas and the Christmas holiday itself. They toasted in the New Year together with some orange juice. 1957 was upon them. There was talk of Gary being posted to Germany, but thankfully at the last minute he was reprieved. It was as if the army captain was watching over them.

They needed to save up to move later in the year, so Margaret found a job doing housework for the officers' wives. Gary was not happy for this arrangement, but knew they needed the money. A lady a few houses along from the bungalow offered to look after Anne for a few hours each week.

The nicest lady Margaret worked for had a beautiful house, and let her play the grand piano for a while after she had finished her work. It had been a long time since she had played. She looked forward to going there. Margaret saved all the money and within a few months had enough for the move, and to put their belongings into storage. There would be no room for their few possessions at her mother's house.

She broached the move to Gary. He was still most unhappy about going to stay with Mrs Trent, but there seemed no other alternative. 'I'll soon find us somewhere once we are there,' he said. So in the autumn when Gary completed his conscripted service they all moved back to Richmond.

******

It started off badly. Gary said he needed transport to get to work, he was fed up with the buses. So he bought a motorbike on hire purchase. Mrs Trent told him in no uncertain terms that you should never buy anything unless you had saved up and bought it outright. She did not believe in hire purchase.

This put Gary's back up. 'Why doesn't she mind her own business?' he cried. 'I told you it would not work coming to live here.' Margaret was very unhappy. Nothing seemed to be going right. They could not find anywhere to live, everything was so expensive. His wages barely covered the money he gave Mrs Trent for their keep and the hire purchase payments soaked up nearly all of the rest of it. Margaret and Gary rowed about money. There was no money to go anywhere or do anything, no money for the necessities for Anne, who was growing fast and needed the next size of baby outfits, and all the time they were couped up with Mrs Trent.

Gary overheard his mother-in-law telling Margaret how stupid she had been to marry him, that he was a loser who would never be able to provide for them. Margaret tried to defend him, saying he just needed a chance and things would get better, but her mother was adamant. 'Why you let that nice chap Sandy through your grasp I will never know.' Yes her mother had liked Sandy, but for reasons she did not understand she had chosen Gary, and she was married to him, so they must make the best of it. She decided to try and find somewhere else for them to live, but had no success.

Gary found another job as a milkman. He passed his test to drive a horse and cart, and was given a milk round just the other side of the river Thames at Teddington. By chance Margaret saw an advertisement in the Lady magazine for a cook/housekeeper at Hampton, not far from Gary's milk round. She went to the phone box and dialled the number. A very well spoken lady answered her call and invited her over to see her. Margaret wrapped Anne up well in her shawl and caught a bus to Hampton, some five miles away.

She was flabbergasted when she saw the house. It was enormous and set in its own grounds. There were vast areas of lawn and shrubs and in the distance she could see from where she stood on the drive a large kitchen garden. She walked up the drive carrying Anne, and rang the doorbell.

The door was opened by a maid, who invited her into the vast hall, and told her to follow her down a long passage to the nursery wing where she was introduced to Mrs White. 'Come in my dear, and sit down.' She turned to the maid and said, 'Would you be kind enough to arrange a tray of tea for us Emily?' The maid nodded and disappeared.

'Now then tell me all about yourself and why you have applied for the job, Mrs Pearce?'

Margaret explained their predicament and that they needed a flat to live in, and that she could only work where she could take the baby. 'In the advertisement you said there was live-in accommodation Mrs White?'

'Yes that is right. We will have a cup of tea and then I will show you round.' 'My husband works in London. He is a Government Minister, and is away a lot, but when he is home, we do entertain. We need someone to cook breakfast every morning and an evening meal six days a week. There is a lady who comes in for a few hours a day and copes with the housework, but she does not wash up I am afraid.' Margaret liked Mrs White, she smiled a lot and appeared very friendly, she was sure Gary would like her.

'I would like to give it a try,' Margaret said. 'I can cook quite well, and I know Anne would be no problem, she seems to sleep for much of the day at the moment, and when she is awake, she sits quite happily in her high chair.'

Emily brought in the tea and it reminded Margaret of when she went to the country with Sandy and had afternoon tea with his mother and father. It reminded her of what her mother had said about Sandy, and how much better off she would be had she continued to see him. Still she loved Gary, although she had to admit he had changed somewhat since they had been married. He never bought her anything, no flowers or chocolates like Sandy had. He never took her anywhere, all he did was work and tinker with his motorbike. He rarely put his arms around her now except for when they were in bed and he wanted sex. That was another thing. He rarely told her he loved her, and often she had to ask him if he still loved her. He became exasperated at times, where had the nice, kind gentle man she had married disappeared to?

Margaret looked around her at this grand house and desperately wanted to live there. She did so hope Mrs White would agree to give her a try. She was sure she could cope, and perhaps if Gary did not live under her mother's roof perhaps things would get better.

CHAPTER 6

Mrs White took Margaret on a grand tour of the house. The ground floor consisted of a long corridor at the front of the house, and along it were various doors. The nursery wing where they started from was used the most. She explained that it was nice and sunny, and when her twelve year old daughter had been smaller, was in constant use. Now she often sat and sewed or read a book there. Mrs White went on to explain that her daughter Caroline was at boarding school at present, but that she came home during the school holidays.

As they proceeded along the corridor Margaret marvelled at the huge pictures on the wall. The first door led into the vast dining room. In the centre of the room was a large refectory table surrounded by many chairs. 'Breakfast is served in here at exactly 7.30am each morning except Sunday when it would be 8am. My husband likes fish for his breakfast, usually kippers or kedgeree, whereas I prefer poached egg on toast, and Caroline prefers cereals, so breakfast is quite an easy informal meal.'

'In the evenings we have a more formal dinner, and I would discuss with you early in the day, or sometimes the day before what would be required. Does that sound all right with you?' she asked. Margaret nodded, it seemed easy enough.

The next room was a small bar room, with a lovely brick fireplace already laid up. The corridor widened then and went past a huge staircase on her left, and in front of her large double doors led into the lounge. It was half the size of a football pitch, she had never seen such a large room before. Lots of sofas, small tables with photographs displayed, and a grand piano. Once more a large ingle nook fireplace took pride of place.

Mrs White explained. 'This room does not get used as often as the nursery wing, although we do entertain quite a bit, and when we do I get Mrs Hughes to come in and help with the preparations and she is very good at setting the table as well as helping prepare the vegetables.' Margaret absorbed this with a feeling of trepidation. She had never prepared food for more than 3-4 people at any one time. Could she do this, she wondered!

They turned and walked up the huge staircase, where she was shown each of the bedrooms. It would seem that Mr White slept on his own at the far end of the upstairs corridor. His room was very sparse with only a single bed and a rather large chest of drawers and wardrobe in the room. The floor was of wooden boards. Caroline on the other hand had a beautiful bedroom next to her mother's rather luxurious room. Margaret's feet sank into thick carpets, and the dressing table was kidney shaped, with frilly chintz curtains to match the curtains at the windows. There were two guest bedrooms, and two bathrooms.

Mrs White took Margaret towards a door at the end of the upstairs corridor and opened it to reveal a small passage along which were two bedrooms and a bathroom. 'This would be your quarters Mrs Pearce, and if you go down those wooden stairs at the end you will come into the back corridor, by the kitchen, where there is a staff lounge for your use.'

'It all looks very nice,' Margaret replied. 'I am sure my husband would like it here.'

'Let us now go and see the kitchen shall we?' She proceeded down the wooden stairs, and turned into the small corridor before they emerged into an enormous kitchen. There were four sinks and an Aga cooker, and simply masses of cupboards. The floor was quarry tiled. 'Goodness the kitchen is very big,' Margaret remarked. 'This house used to be owned by Jessie Matthews and her husband Sonny Hale,' Mrs White explained, 'and they entertained quite a lot I believe.' Margaret was agog. She knew of Jessie Matthews, she sang on the radio and was on the stage in London. Wow!

'If we go out of the back door and past the garages we will come into the vegetable garden. The gardener keeps us well supplied with all sorts of vegetables from potatoes to asparagus, tomatoes, beans and cabbages. You just come and help yourself to whatever you need, and Mrs Pearce you can also utilise any of the stocks for your own use.'

'Really?' Margaret exclaimed. *How lovely fresh vegetables, and free,* she thought.

They returned to the nursery wing and Mrs White told her that they were quite desperate for someone to start, and asked if she could move in by the following week.

'I am sure that will be possible. I will talk to my husband tonight, and will telephone you tomorrow. I am sure there will not be a problem,' she said as she got up to leave.

That evening she explained about her visit to Hampton to Gary. He was thrilled that they could move nearer to where he worked, and also leave her mother's house. He could not foresee a problem. So arrangements were made to move their few items of furniture which were still in store to Hampton. Mrs Trent did not seem happy about the arrangements, and Margaret knew her mother would miss Anne dreadfully, although she said nothing.

So a week later on a bright sunny day, they hired a small van and moved their things into the servants quarters of the big house.

******

Gary was most impressed with the big house, and liked their quarters too. She introduced him to Mrs White, who he said was a very nice lady. Within a few days Margaret started her cooking duties. Fortunately she was able to have Anne with her most of the time, although Anne slept quite a lot, which made life easy for her to prepare things for the evening meal during the afternoon, while Anne slept.

Mrs White suggested to Margaret that she made early morning trays of tea for both herself and her husband, and put them outside their respective bedroom doors at 7am each morning. She was happy with this. She had as yet to meet Mr White, he was not at home much during the week. Mrs White explained he had an apartment in town, meaning London. 'How very odd,' she thought.

When Gary heard about her taking a tray of tea up to Mr White, he voiced his disapproval. 'I don't think you should have to do that,' he cried. 'I don't mind you taking it up for the lady but not him.' He ranted.

'Oh Gary, stop fussing it is quite all right and I don't mind, honest.'

Gary persisted. 'He might drag you into his bedroom.'

'Oh don't be so stupid, of course he won't,' she replied. 'I have never seen him yet.' Still Gary was not pleased with the arrangement, and often moaned about it. Margaret tried to take no notice, but it upset her that he did not trust her or Mr White.

She soon fell into a routine. Breakfast was easy, and the first time she took breakfast into the big dining room, she was introduced to Mr White. He was a big round man about fifty years of age, with a very red face. He shook hands with Margaret. She liked him, she thought, he looked very kind, and seemed interested in her. He was old enough to be her father, she laughed at the thoughts of what Gary had said about him.

Life was good. No rent to pay, no vegetables to buy, and no arguments between Gary and her mother. Gary's wages were adequate, so things were looking up.

Margaret saw very little of Emily the maid, who appeared to spend a lot of time upstairs sorting and mending clothes for Mrs White and her daughter Caroline, who as yet Margaret had not seen. Emily always answered the front door when the bell rang and the only time Emily made her presence known was if she came into the kitchen to make up a tea tray for Mrs White and her friends during the course of the day.

CHAPTER 7

Margaret loved the small lounge, which doubled as a dining room as well. It was cosy and it was so nice after living at her mother's house, where there had been no privacy. The room was fully furnished, with a round table with four chairs, and two comfortable armchairs near the fireplace. There was a large sideboard along one wall and large cupboards along another. The room was right next door to the kitchen, where the Aga with its four big ovens were always hot, so it kept the lounge cosily warm, and there was no need for her to light the fire. However in the summer the windows were always open to let out the heat.

Each day she would be told by Mrs White what to cook for the evening meal, and she would go down into the kitchen garden and select the vegetables. Although she had not enjoyed a very good relationship with her mother, she had learnt how to cook. Her mother had been a cook at the East India Docks canteen in London before she had married her father. History was repeating itself, she thought.

The butcher's boy would arrive on his bicycle mid morning and she would prepare the meat for the evening meal whilst Anne slept, usually waking about noon. This gave Margaret time to feed the child, before taking her for a walk in her pram. Gary left early each morning to complete his milk round, returning just after lunch, and after having a wash would usually sleep for an hour. It all worked like clockwork. Gary bought a sidecar for the motorbike so that he could take both her and Anne out into the country, where they would go for walks or feed ducks.

The only fly in the ointment was Gary's continual moaning about Mr White. Gary, for some reason, did not like him. She felt sure that Gary was jealous of him, but why? He was a very friendly man, who always thanked her

for anything she did for him. She tried to take no notice, but was constantly reminded not to go into Mr White's bedroom, when she took his tea tray up
in the mornings.

Mr White liked cooking, and often came into the kitchen when he was at home and would cook himself some lunch. Gary came home early one day and through the large windows of the kitchen he saw Mr White with his arm on Margaret's shoulder. She had been preparing the fish for the evening meal and Anne was still asleep. All Mr White was doing was watching over her shoulder and commenting on her skill at filleting the fish. All afternoon Gary ranted and raged.

'Oh Gary please be quiet,' she begged him. 'Mr and Mrs White will hear you and I don't want to lose this job.' Tears came to her eyes.

'I am sure you don't,' he shouted. 'You wouldn't want to upset your fancy man would you?' he jeered.

'Gary, he is not my fancy man, I work here and he was only watching what I was doing.' She knew she was getting upset. Gary stormed out, started up his Royal Enfield motorcycle and roared down the drive. He was gone for the rest of the day. She had put his dinner in the oven to keep warm, but when he finally returned about 9 o'clock he said he did not want it, and went upstairs to bed. Margaret did not know what to do. Should she follow him and say sorry, but for what? She decided to do the ironing, and eventually went to bed about 10.30pm. Gary was still awake. She had not put the light on, but she knew he was watching her.

'Come here,' he demanded. She walked over to the bed, she was half undressed. He pulled her down onto the bed, and kissed her hard. It hurt, he moved on top of her and jeered. 'Is this what you want?' and grabbed her by the shoulder and propelled himself on top of her, entering her roughly, and made her cry out. 'Gary you are hurting me.'

'Perhaps I don't give you enough,' he whispered into her ear. 'We'll soon alter that.' Tears sprang to her eyes, how could he be so awful, he was supposed to love her, wasn't he? She endured his treatment of her, and when he finally fell asleep, she lay curled up in the bed and cried.

She woke the next morning with sore red eyes and feeling sore everywhere. She got up and took a bath. Gary had already left for work. She sank into the warm water and thought about the previous day. Had she done anything wrong? Then she suddenly remembered she had not put her cap in. *Oh Lord please don't let me become pregnant again yet* she thought. She did not want to leave this lovely house.

That morning Mrs White had noticed how quiet Margaret was, and also the red rimmed eyes. However, she said nothing. She asked her to pick some flowers and arrange them on the table for dinner that night. They were entertaining another couple for a meal at 7.30pm. 'I have written out the menu my dear, something quite simple, but we will need you to wait at table as well. Major Blake and his wife are very good friends of ours.'

Margaret decided she would have to ask Gary to mind Anne while she was so busy that evening. When Gary came home he was still very off hand. She plucked up courage and without commenting on the previous evening, she asked him if he would mind Anne for a couple of hours, and bathe the child and get her ready for bed.

'Yes, all right,' he replied, 'but I hope this does not happen often. I like to have my dinner and have a rest in the evenings,' he remarked.

Whew, he had agreed! He looked at her sheepishly, and went and put his arm round her and said, 'I am sorry I lost my temper last night.'

'It's all right,' she replied.

True to his word he looked after Anne, and Margaret had her first taste of cooking a four course meal and serving it as well. Major Blake was a very rotund man who seemed to bellow when he spoke, but was very jolly, whereas his wife was a very meek woman who seemed to agree with everything. After the meal, they all went off to the big lounge, where the two men could be heard roaring with laughter.

Margaret was busy washing up when Mrs White came into the kitchen and said, 'That was a very nice meal my dear, thank you very much.'

'I'm glad you liked it,' she replied. With her heart singing, she went back into their lounge where both Gary and Anne had fallen asleep. It was late, nearly 10 o'clock, she picked up Anne and took her upstairs and placed her into her cot. When she returned downstairs, Gary was still fast asleep, she decided to leave him there, and went to bed herself. She did not see him until the following afternoon, when he remarked that she should have woken him and he could have gone to bed.

Two months later, Margaret realised she was pregnant. She had not felt sick like when she had been expecting Anne, but she was very tired. She felt devastated, she would not be allowed to stay at the big house now, how long before she had to tell Mrs White? She dreaded it, now where would they go? That evening she told Gary the news. She had expected him to be pleased, because he had always wanted a son, but she was not prepared for his response.

'Pregnant!' he yelled, 'How did you become pregnant? You always use that cap thing don't you?'

'Yes Gary I do, but it probably happened one night when I forgot to put it in.'

He walked up and down, and she could see he was losing his temper. 'I suppose it's his,' he glared at her.

'I don't know what you mean,' she replied. 'Who's?'

'Why that ponce of course, your fancy man.'

'Gary you don't mean Mr White, how could you?' she exclaimed. 'He is very kind but honestly this child is yours.'

'I bet, well it is not mine.' And with that he went out slamming the door behind him. Margaret was beside herself. The tears which had welled up now overflowed down her cheeks. If only Wilma was there to cuddle and talk to, she thought. How could she prove the baby was Gary's? Why was he being so awful to her?

He sulked for days and she herself was very unhappy. But there was little she could do except carry on. Five days passed before he started to talk to her again. She kept out of Mr White's way as much as possible, and was able to explain to Gary that they would have to find somewhere else to live shortly.

'I will not tell Mrs White for a few weeks yet, which will give us time to find a flat or something.'

'As long as we are not going back to your mother's,' he replied.

A few weeks later he came in grinning all over his face. 'I have found us somewhere to live,' he bragged.

'Really,' she was pleased 'Where is that Gary?'

'One of my customers owns a flat in Brixton in London, and will let us have it for a low rent.'

'But Gary you will have to give up your job,' her anxiety growing.

'I know, but I will soon get another in London, you'll see,' he replied. She was not so sure. Jobs were at a premium. Later that week he took them in the sidecar up to Brixton to look at the flat. It was just off Herne Hill. It was a very tall house, and she soon learned that the flat which was available was on the top floor, three floors up. They climbed the stairs, and were shown round by the lady who lived in the bottom flat. She told them her name was Mrs Williams. 'It's only two rooms,' she said, 'and it will need some decorating, but the good thing it is not expensive.'

Margaret was puffing by the time they were on the top floor. The back room had a small black range, and an old gas cooker stood in the corner, as well as a stone sink with a brass tap. The lights were gas mantles. How horrid she thought. They went up three more steps to the bedroom, which was empty except for an old iron framed double bed. There were bare floorboards. 'There is a bathroom one floor down, and a toilet, but you have to share it with Mr and Mrs Green who live on that floor,' she told them.

'Where will I put Anne's pram?' Margaret asked.

'Well you can't keep it in the hallway, it will be in the way, you will have to bring it up here.' She replied.

When Mrs Williams left them and went downstairs, Margaret exploded. 'Gary I cannot live here.'

'Calm down,' it will only be for a short while to give us time to find something better.' He said.

'Gary you are not listening. I cannot live here,' she reiterated. But he had already decided they would have to make the best of it. 'We will decorate the walls and clean up the cooker, and bring our things, and you will see it in a different light.'

Margaret was so unhappy. She would be leaving that lovely house in Hampton for this. She was adamant she would find something else. Unfortunately anything she found they could not afford, and two weeks later agreed to move to Brixton.

She told Mrs White, they would have to leave because of a new baby. How kind she had been and said she was sorry to see them go, especially Margaret who she had come to rely on so much.

So once more Margaret packed up all their belongings and they hired a van to take their few possessions to Brixton.

CHAPTER 8

Margaret piled their clothes on the bare floor in the bedroom, there were no cupboards, and no chest of drawers to put them in. how she missed the lovely house at Hampton with its fitted cupboards. There was no money to purchase any furniture, so they would have to make do. Gary had said it was only temporary, so they would have to manage.

There was no room for Anne's cot in the bedroom either, so they placed it in the corner of the living room. Margaret set to work and cleaned the range, and the sink. They had obviously not been used for a while. Then Gary started stripping off the wallpaper. The awful old brown paper came off, but he also found there were about five other layers of wallpaper underneath. It was a marathon task. From the small amount of money they had saved whilst she had been working at the big house, they bought five rolls of wallpaper in a pretty pale green shade so as to lighten the room. The walls were so badly pitted, there was no way they could paint them.

Anne had watched them stripping the wallpaper, and although she was only very small, she had recently started getting into everything. Now she was up on her feet and toddling about she enjoyed 'helping'. She followed Gary round and pulled at the paper on the wall, tearing off small bits. She thought it great fun. Unfortunately when Gary started to paste the new paper onto the wall, Anne came behind him and started tearing it off as well.

'Can't you keep that child away?' he shouted, 'She has ruined two sheets, and now I will have to buy another roll of wallpaper.' Anne started to cry, she did not like her father shouting, it frightened her. There was nowhere else to go only the bedroom, so Margaret took her out for a walk. She was glad her mother had bought a pushchair for the child, it was so much easier to get up and down the three

47

flights of stairs. They walked along Coldharbour Lane and along to Camberwell. It took quite a while, giving Gary time to finish the task.

They stopped at the fish and chip shop on the way home, and bought some fish and chips for supper. Margaret left the pushchair with Anne in outside the shop. Soon she heard the child screaming, and went outside to find a West Indian lady trying to talk to Anne, who had never seen a black person before. It obviously frightened her. Margaret picked her up and carried her into the shop, and waited for their food, before coaxing the child back into the pushchair to go back to the flat. She told Gary what had happened.

He laughed and said, 'She will get used to it, there are lots of West Indian people living here.'

'I hope we are not going to live here for very long,' she said. 'What with the stairs, and the cramped conditions, and now if we go out Anne is going to be frightened all the time.' She hated the flat.

It took the best part of two weeks to clean up the two rooms. Washing was a problem, there was nowhere to hang the washing to dry. She washed their clothes and the nappies daily by hand. She noticed other people in top flats had a pole which they pushed out of the back window, and a washing line was attached. It was rather precarious, but it worked. Gary applied for a job with the local dairy, and soon had a milk round. They needed every penny of what he earned to live on, what with paying the rent, and buying all their food, it soon disappeared. How were they ever going to find somewhere better? She was continually buying gas mantles for the gas lights, as they broke very easily, and it was heavy work bringing up a bag of coal or logs for the range.

One day she was walking along with Anne in the pushchair, when she saw a advertisement on a door.

OUTWORKERS REQUIRED, GOOD MACHINISTS NEEDED URGENTLY. She had the sewing machine her mother had bought her for her 21st birthday, she could work at home and still look after Anne, she thought. She went inside and enquired. A very nice man interviewed her and said he would give her a try. A van would deliver 50 blouses which needed all the seams sewing, she would get 1s 3d a blouse. Wow! She knew she could do that.

Gary was not much pleased when she told him, but had to agree the money would come in useful, so she started work. She gradually worked up to 200 blouses a week. The factory were very pleased with her work, and she could at last start to save some money. Her body was getting bigger and bigger as the weeks went on, and it was uncomfortable at times continually sitting at the machine, but she had set herself a goal - to leave the flat. She went to the council offices and put their names down for council housing, but she was warned it could be a very long wait.

Because of the shortage of hospital beds, she was still booked to have her second baby at Kingston Hospital near where her mother lived. Gary took her for her antenatal appointments, and as the birth got nearer these visits became more frequent. Her back started to ache and she knew the birth was imminent.

Her mother had agreed to have Anne when she went into hospital, and at the beginning of February Margaret took Anne to her mother's and said a tearful farewell. Two days later she was admitted to the hospital and then the pains stopped. As she lived so far from the hospital, they kept her in, and gave her some caster oil and orange juice to drink. It tasted foul, and made her feel sick, but a little while later the birth pains started again. She helped around the ward, giving out tea and coffee to other mothers, and helped the nursing staff with all manners of tasks, and all the while the labour pains got worse, but because they were so busy, they did not realise Margaret was about to give birth, until she shouted that she wanted to push. Suddenly she was rushed upstairs to the labour ward, and within fifteen minutes, her baby son was born.

Peter was a big baby, weighing in at 8lb 12oz. He was just perfect. She cried with joy, the birth had been so easy too. It was by then 2am in the morning. She was so elated, and could not wait for Gary to see his son. She slept for a few hours, before being woken to feed the baby. She had to wait all day to see Gary, but dutifully at 7pm he arrived for the visiting hour. He brought with him a bunch of pink tulips. He had already been to the nursery to see the baby. 'Isn't he lovely, Gary?' she asked.

'He is very big, I do not think I could have produced such a large baby.' He glared at her, 'He's more likely to be Mr White's baby.'

Margaret looked at him dumbfounded. 'Gary how could you say such a thing, of course he is our child.' Tears welled in her eyes. How could Gary think Mr White was the father, why he was an old man, to them. They hardly spoke during visiting time, Gary appeared to be sulking. The nurse came along and took the flowers and put them in a vase, which she placed on the trolley table at the foot of the bed.

'I'm going to call him Peter,' she said at last.

'Fine,' he replied, and continued to sit looking round the ward. Eventually he left, not even kissing her goodbye. Margaret sat and cried. What was the matter with Gary? Why was he always accusing her of things she had not done? Little was she to know, this was just the beginning of his possessive, jealous nature, which she was to endure for many years.

The tulips all keeled over, and hung down the vase, which was just how she felt. Other mother's flowers looked lovely, hers looked awful. She had lots of milk, and because it was so prolific she expressed some to be given to premature twins which had just been born by caesarean and the mother did not have any milk to give them. The nursing staff praised her up, knowing she was rather depressed. They told her it was normal to be down after giving birth, but Margaret knew it had nothing to do with that, it was because of Gary, and his treatment of her.

When she left the hospital some ten days later, she was delighted that her figure was almost back to normal, and she could get into her clothes quite easily. Her mother had given Gary a carrycot, which she had bought for the new baby. They placed the child into the soft blankets for it was quite cold outside, and took the bus to her mother's. Gary held the cot, as she raced down the garden path and scooped Anne up into her arms. How she had missed her. What a wonderful day. Gary's motorbike and sidecar were outside the house. There is no way they would be able to get the carrycot into the sidecar as well as herself and the two children.

The next day her mother's next door neighbour who owned a car offered to drive the little family back to Brixton. Gary rode the motorbike back. It was the solution. Margaret expressed her gratitude, but Gary did not like the fact that she would be sitting next to Mr Laing for the journey home.

However, they arrived back at the flat late that afternoon, with a baby demanding to be fed, and Anne wanting to sit on her lap, and Gary wanting his dinner. She felt totally overwhelmed. It took quite some weeks to make a new routine. Peter seemed such a hungry baby and needed feeding often or he would wail. Anne became jealous of the baby because Margaret was always feeding him or bathing him, or changing his nappy. Gary obviously felt pushed out, and sulked a lot.

She needed to earn some more money. Gary wanted a car now there were so many of them. 'Just a cheap one will do,' he remarked. Cheap it would have to be. There was £20 in the savings kitty, and she had earmarked that money for getting out of the flat. At a house on his milk round he came across an old Jowett, which smoked a bit, but the man who owned it said Gary could have it for £10. So she gave him the money.

She went to see the manager Mr Grey at the clothes factory, and told him she needed to start back sewing again. He was delighted, and soon she was machining 100 blouses a week. Margaret ensured the children had a sleep each afternoon, when she could do lots of blouses as well as after they had gone to bed. Gary however, was not happy with this arrangement. He had to go to bed early so that he could get up at 5am for his milk round and was put out that his needs could not be met. Margaret was too busy and the only time they had time for each other was during the night, with Gary grinding on top of her until he was sated and she felt used. He never told her he loved her, and she felt quite sure all he wanted her for was sex.

It made her more determined that she was going to leave the flat. Her output to the clothing factory increased to 150 a week, and soon she had £35 saved. She convinced Gary to go up to the Ideal Home Exhibition in London. She had read that there were houses being built outside of London, in the country, and you only needed a small deposit to secure one.

'I would much rather wait for a council house,' Gary said.

'Well the council said it would be a very long wait, and I am not prepared to wait that long,' she replied. 'I cannot bear living here in Brixton, and in this awful flat.' So the following week they went up to the exhibition, where after much walking round they found the firm offering the low deposits. They gave them all the information, and an appointment to view one of the properties in Harmsworth in Hampshire the following week.

Back at the flat, she worked out she had £25 for the deposit, and £5 to hire a van, the only fly in the ointment was the solicitors fee of £20. She didn't sleep that night, she kept thinking, 'where can I get £20?' She could not ask her mother, but an idea struck her, she could ask Ted, her mother's partner. Yes that was it, she would borrow the money from him, if he would agree, and she would find work in Harmsworth and pay him back. She felt much better. She would go and see her mother the following weekend and talk to Ted, her mother's partner. She was sure he would help her.

The following Sunday they set off together in the car for Ham, and were welcomed into the house by her mother. Mrs Pearce was still quite cool to Gary and she herself did not fare much better, but her mother adored the children. Gary went out to tinker with the car, which gave her the opportunity to talk to Ted. He was down at the bottom of the garden by himself. She slipped quietly out of the house and walked down the garden to where Ted was working hard clearing some weeds.

'Hi Ted can I talk to you for a few minutes?' she asked.

'Yes my dear what can I do for you?' He always smiled nicely at her, and she quite liked him, but hated it when he called her 'duck'.

She told him about the houses being built in Hampshire and the total cost of the house would be £2025, which she felt they could get a mortgage for. That she had the deposit, but she could not manage the solicitors fees. Ted appeared to think this over for a little while, before saying, 'All right, I'll agree to lend you £20, and I suggest you pay me back at say £4 a month, how does that sound?' he asked.

'That would be great, but don't tell Mum will you?' she replied.

'No, all right it's just between you and me.'

How wonderful. She would not tell Gary, let him think she had enough money. So the following week they went to Harmsworth and looked at the showhouse. A three bedroom semi-detached house, with a kitchen, bathroom, and a long lounge diner. The plot would include a fair size garden. Margaret was excited, even Gary looked pleased at the prospect.

He assured Margaret it would not take him long to find a job, probably a local dairy. The agent said the house which they wished to earmark would be ready in four weeks time, time enough to get a solicitor and a mortgage. At last there was a light at the end of the tunnel, they could leave that beastly flat and start off in a new house, in a new area with their family and maybe things would get better between herself and Gary.

Margaret worked really hard over the next few weeks, she knew there was furniture to buy, a single bed for Anne, and a double bed for themselves. They would need a chest of drawers and a cooker, and they would have to buy some carpeting. *What had she taken on!* But nothing could dull her spirit. With the children being a little easier now and not quite so demanding, she was able to take on 200 blouses a week. Mr Grey was not happy to hear she was leaving the area, but wished her well. She raised a further £15, and worked out she could afford a cheap cooker and a secondhand bed for Anne as well as two chests of drawers. The carpets would have to wait.

So on a warm summer day in 1958 the family moved to Harmsworth.

CHAPTER 9

They arrived at the same time as the van, and tried to get into their new house. It was locked. Being a Saturday afternoon, nobody was about. They could not get in. The van driver was anxious to unload and get on his way back to London. 'Gary what can we do?' she asked.

'I have no idea, you tell me, after all it was your idea to buy this house.'

Margaret was wondering what they could do. She left Gary with the children and walked up to the showhouse. Inside was a man, she knocked on the door, and she explained to him that they were trying to move in.

'I am sorry, but we have not had the go ahead from your solicitor, and we have not received the deposit,' he told her.

'But I paid the deposit last week, and the solicitor told us to arrange a day to move in, I did telephone and speak to the site foreman, and agreed on today,' she replied.

'I am sorry, but the site foreman is not here today, and I cannot give you permission to move in, I am only the sales rep.' He appeared to be dismissing her.

'Look we have all our possessions in the removal van and the men just want to unload and get back to London, please can we put our things in the house?' She was thinking 'Where on earth will we all sleep tonight?'

The man finally capitulated and went and found a key, and went and unlocked the front door of their house. 'You can put your things in, but I cannot let you stay there, that would be possession, and I am not authorised to let you.'

'All right, thanks.' Margaret was relieved, but it was only a few minutes later that Gary poked her in the arm and said, 'A great idea of yours wasn't it, now where do we sleep, in the car I suppose? There will be no one here tomorrow on a Sunday either.'

Margaret did not need telling. She was mortified. It was bad enough the cooker would not be there until Monday, and the cot and beds would need making up, she felt so miserable, and Gary was not helping. Blaming her as usual if anything went wrong.

The sales rep locked the front door behind the removal men, and they watched them all depart. Gary slunk off round the back of the house, and came back looking quite cheerful. 'Let us go and get something to eat, I have a plan.'

They drove into the small market town, and found a café, where they had some food. As it started to get dark, they once more got back into the car. Gary drove to the house, and again went round the back. A few minutes later he opened the front door.

'How did you do that?' Margaret asked.

'Easy, the window to the kitchen wasn't latched properly, and I put a piece of card through and lifted the latch, so we can stay here for the weekend, and hopefully get sorted out on Monday.'

She was dubious that they should have broken into the house, or that they should stay, but needs must she thought. They took the children in and while she sorted out some bed linen, and then fed Peter, Gary assembled the cot and the single bed for Anne. By the time the children were in bed and asleep, they were both really tired and could not contemplate putting up the double bed, not only that it would make too much noise and wake the children. So they slept on the hard wooden floor of the lounge.

Sunday morning, after feeding the two children and salvaging the flask of coffee from the car for themselves, they put up and assembled the double bed. Every bone in her body ached, sleeping on the hard floor had been so uncomfortable. They had to go out for dinner and brought back their flasks which had been filled, as well as milk and sandwiches for the evening.

On Monday morning, the site became very noisy early with builders and dumper trucks going up and down the road. They got dressed, and Margaret went out to find the foreman. He was astounded that they had stayed in the house for the weekend, and did not appear too pleased, but having listened to her story, he agreed they could stay provided that the cheque for the deposit was transferred to their solicitor that day. So later that morning she had taken a bus into town, and called on the solicitor, leaving Gary to mind the children at the house. The solicitor agreed to complete the sale that day, much to her relief. She returned back home, with some fresh food, to find the cooker being delivered. Things were looking up. With the cooker connected she could cook their meals.

Anne loved making lots of noise by running around on the bare boards, which drove Gary to distraction at times, but it also tired her out. In town they found a secondhand shop and bought a few cheap items, a table and chairs, and an old divan settee. But they were in their own house, now it just left Gary to find a job. He had been promised a job at the local dairy before they moved, but when Gary went to see them they told him the position was already filled. Eventually he found a job as a salesman for a provident company, selling household goods and clothing door to door. He admitted he was not good at selling but would give it a go. They survived for many weeks on his basic salary plus a small amount of commission, so they were able to pay the mortgage and eat.

Margaret could find no suitable work at first, but on an impulse, she visited all the tailors shops in town and offered to do alterations for them. It was a slow beginning, but gradually the volume of work increased. What would she do without her sewing machine. Her thoughts often wandered back thinking of what she had wanted to do, become a welfare officer and work with children. There was not time for studying now, all her time was used up sewing, or looking after the children and Gary.

One day she was talking to the foreman on the site, and he told her that his daughter was getting married, but she could not afford an expensive wedding dress.

'Why not let me make one for her it would be so much cheaper?' she volunteered.

'Could you?' he replied.

'Well I can sew quite well, I am sure I could do it.' She said, so it was agreed that his daughter would come down and talk to her about it.

She had never made anything so grand, but she felt positive she could do it, and do it she did. What a beautiful design the girl chose, and brought yards of ice white satin, and tulle. It took the best part of three weeks to finish, with most of the sewing done after the children were in bed, she did not want anyone putting sticky fingers on the dress. After two fitting s she finally completed the final touches, and covered the dress in plastic. She charged the girl £20 for her work, and was delighted when she was given another pound tip on top. Her first customer was very pleased.

That night she told Gary about her good fortune. 'Oh good, we need to change the car, this one needs a lot of money spent on it.' Within a week he had found an SS Jaguar, for just £15. It was quite old, but very strong. It also used lots of petrol.

She had wanted the money for other things as well as ensuring she could afford their electricity bill. Well she would have to make some more money for sure. So she had advertised locally that she made wedding dresses and bridesmaids dresses. She was soon inundated with orders and had to select just a few, but from then on she felt they had turned the corner.

Unfortunately Gary's attempts at selling were not proving good, and it was not long before he was given the sack. It was two weeks before he found another job, delivering meat from a butchers shop in town to people just outside of the town. It was poorly paid, but was a job, and they were given a free joint of meat each week for the Sunday roast. So effectively Margaret became the breadwinner. Word spread of her talent at making inexpensive wedding attire, and so she sat and sewed, and her eyes became sore and tired, but she could not let up, not now, there was the mortgage to pay and money to pay back to Ted. She started hiring wedding dresses.

Margaret knew she needed to advertise the wedding hire business. She made quite a bit of profit for each hiring, but had little sewing to do, just adjustments for each girl who came to her.

She saw an article in a daily paper showing a bride walking down the catwalk at a London Fashion Show. '*If only I could do something like that*' she thought. But it had kindled an idea. She asked around and found she could hire the local college hall for a small sum of money. She had all the dresses hanging up in her room, but how to organise a mannequin parade. She drew designs and numbered the dresses she was considering showing, then she contacted some of the girls she knew who had hired dresses and lured them into contemplating modelling the dresses for her. Now all she had to do was arrange to advertise. She needed a theme or something to interest people to coming. Margaret put on her thinking cap and decided she needed a personality to be present as a guest. '*I know,*' she thought,

'*A mystery guest*' but who? She asked around and someone suggested she contact an agency in London.

With luck on her side she found an agency who would provide a celebrity for an evening for £25 appearance money. Whew what a lot of money, but then if business improved it would be worth it. So she booked it. Two days later she was told that actress and radio personality, Avril Angers, would be able to come. So she advertised in the local paper that a Mannequin Parade was to be held at the College at 7pm two weeks later. She pointed out to Gary that a car would have to collect Miss Angers at the railway station a little after 6pm. He immediately decided he would do it in his own car. Margaret would have preferred to have hired a nice car to collect her with a uniformed chauffeur, but she had to go along with Gary.

The show was a huge success. The local Mayoress Mrs Peet attended, looking pleased to be sitting next to Avril Angers. Margaret felt very proud of all the girls who did a fine job parading the dresses along the catwalk, which had been created by the college caretaker. The show lasted an hour and a half. It was mooted that Miss Angers expected to be taken for a meal. Oh Lord what could she do, she had all the dresses to take back home and the hall to clear. One of the girls mothers who liked being in charge said she would be happy to take Miss Angers to a local hotel and buy her a meal and take her back to the railway station afterwards. 'Oh would you?' Margaret cried, ' that would be so helpful.' All her muscles ached, it had been a long day, and she was looking forward to relaxing in a hot bath once the children were in bed. What an incredible day, but it had been worth it, and within days orders came in thick and fast.

Over the next two years she progressed, but Gary resented the fact she earned more than him. He often made spiteful remarks to upset her, but she steeled herself to take little notice, but inwardly her heart was sad. What more could she do? Gary had no training for work, all he knew about were motorbikes and delivering milk. Even when he had been working on a milk round she had always worked his books out for him, he could never balance them.

The final straw came at the end of 1960 when she discovered that she was pregnant again. How on earth could she manage? As her pregnancy progressed, she worked harder and harder, she was churning out three wedding dresses a week. The lady who lived across the road needed a small part time job, so Margaret hired her to stitch hems and sew on buttons. She liked Emma, who was also useful keeping an eye on the children, and would often take them for a walk whilst she got on. She started to make up some wedding dresses and keep them spare, and eventually started to hire them for a fraction of the cost. She found she could hire a dress three or four times, ensuring it was cleaned between hirings. She put Emma in charge of this.

It was a hot summer in 1961 and she always felt hot, she was also very fat with baby, and getting down on the floor to adjust a hem was agony, but she managed.

That year her mother and Ted decided to move to Harmsworth. Mrs Trent had found a bungalow being built in the nearby village of Tamping. It was being sold for £2600, and with the sale of the house in Ham they could well afford it. Her mother told her the bungalow would be finished before the baby was born, and it was.

As summer turned to autumn Margaret had to give up work, and live off Gary's wage. Her blood pressure was sky high, and the doctor was threatening to put her into hospital. Her feet and ankles swelled to enormous proportions, and eventually she gave birth to a baby girl in October, the day after her own birthday. They called her Sarah.

For some unknown reason Anne was very jealous of this baby, and often pinched the baby and made it cry. So she bought Anne a lifelike doll and dolls pram so that she could play at being mummy herself, but Anne was having none of it, she wanted a real baby to play with. It did not help that Anne started school that term, and felt pushed out with the baby taking her place at home.

The bills were piling up and with another baby to care for, there was very little time for sewing. The day revolved around getting all the children ready by 8.30 so that she could walk Anne to school, as well as keeping Peter amused. Go home, feed and bath the baby, and tidy up indoors.

Get the lunch ready, feed the baby and walk back to the school and collect Anne, then prepare the dinner for Gary and the children before getting them all ready for bed. It was a nightmare. However, it gradually became routine, and as the baby grew she started to take in some sewing. Only a little at first, but gradually she increased it with the help of Emma. The hired dresses were increasing, and within six months they were hiring dresses and bridesmaids dresses every week.

They bought a single bed for Peter as Sarah needed the cot, having outgrown the carrycot. During the following year the butchers shop closed down so Gary was once more unemployed. It was some weeks before he acquired a part time job driving private hire taxis. He started buying parts for the car to keep it going, and some electrical goods he fancied, on a have now pay later regime. He seemed to do this to spite her, the more she tried to keep their heads above water, the more money he wasted. When she challenged him about it, he would punch her or threaten her in some way, she never came off best.

In 1963 she decided she would have to turn things around, Gary would have to appear to earn more than her. He could drive cars, and sometimes he drove a funeral or wedding car for a local car hire firm, as well as the private hire driving. This gave her an idea. She had a bit of money saved unbeknown to Gary, but they were two months in arrears with the mortgage. She had paid Ted back all the money she owed him, but the building society wanted three months money or they would evict them.

She decided to put the house on the market. It was now worth £2600. She had seen a house advertised with three bedrooms not far from where they lived for sale at £2200 and as it needed some work doing on it, she could try making an offer. She was in luck, the couple wanted to move quickly as they might lose the house they wanted in Devon. They would accept £2000. Oh great she thought, that will leave me the money to pay off the building society, and buy some more furniture.

A buyer came forward offering the exact price they were asking, so she went for it, and within two months they had moved.

CHAPTER 10

Gary knew they had to go along with the sale, there had been no other choice, although he did not enjoy the upheaval of moving. They moved their sparse amount of furniture into the house they had just bought. It was such an old house, which had been two cottages knocked into one. Steep stairs led up to the small landing. There were three small bedrooms and a bathroom. Downstairs there was a fairly large lounge and a kitchen, and on the opposite end of the staircase was another room which she decided she could use for her dressmaking and dress hire.

'And who is going to do all the repairs needed, and redecorate Madam?' he challenged her.

'Well Gary as you are only working part time at present I thought perhaps you could make a start on it, I will help where I can,' she replied.

'And what can you do?' he retorted.

'I am not sure,' she replied, 'but I will do all I can to make the house pleasant to live in,' she walked off into the kitchen, and started to stoke the boiler. There was a coalhouse right next to the kitchen, and a coal scuttle just by the boiler. It was not ideal, but it did not take long to get the boiler roaring and the water piping hot. She spent some days washing paintwork, and the sinks and bath. The tiles in the bathroom were very greasy, but before long she had them shining.

She realised they could not continue, even with a smaller mortgage, with Gary working only partial hours. There was about £100 left over once everything was settled. She had a thought, *'Gary could work for himself.'* If she bought a decent car, or maybe two, they could set up a hire company, and Gary could drive. That night she broached the idea to him. 'We could sell the Jaguar, which is unsuitable, and buy two large cars for private hire taxis, which could also be used for weddings,' she ventured.

Gary sat listening to her, he was very quiet. He liked the Jaguar, but it was costing a lot to keep it on the road, it was so old. 'Okay, so we buy some different cars, but how will we get started?' he said.

'Well we would have to advertise until we become known, I can draw up an advert and place it in the local Gazette.' She watched him coming to terms with the idea.

'All right, let us go and look for some cars,' he said.

So the following day, with the house still in a muddle, they set off with the children in the Jaguar to look for some suitable cars which they could afford. In the next village they found a garage which had just the right sort of cars, Humber Hawks, good strong cars, both black in colour.

'How much are you asking for the Humbers?' Gary enquired. The man came forward in greasy overalls rubbing his hands with an oily rag. 'I'll take £50 each,' he said.

'How much for both of them?' Margaret asked. The man looked her up and down, and proceeded to tell her they were in very good condition so he could not suggest much less, as there would be no profit for him.

'I'll give you £80 for the two,' she proposed.

'No lady, I cannot go that low,' he thought for a minute then said, 'I'll accept £85 for the two.'

'Okay we'll take them,' Margaret got out her wallet and proceeded to give the man the money. They made arrangements to collect the cars later in the week.

Gary was thrilled, and later that day, she wrote out advertisements firstly for the Jaguar, and secondly one advertising the hire car business, which would be opening in two weeks. This gave them time to sort out the cars and also the muddle at the house. Gary found a friend of his to go with him to pick up the cars from the garage, while she set up her sewing machine in the spare room downstairs. They quickly sold the Jaguar for more than they paid for it which was brilliant.

Her brother John and his wife Elsa came to visit, and John offered to put up a long hanging rail for the wedding dresses she was to hire. She was over the moon. John was very clever with his hands, and a week later he came over on his own and started work. The dresses were all laid out upstairs in their polythene wrappers. When he had finished, she brought them down and arranged them tidily on the rail. Her previous customers soon found where she lived, and within a very short space of time she was terribly busy. Gary had not liked John coming over and helping, he did not like John very much, and the feeling was mutual.

Anne changed school when they moved to the little village and in 1963 Peter started school too. He felt very important going to school that first day. He waved her goodbye at the school gate, and ran along with Anne into the building. He told her all about his day that evening whilst she was cooking the dinner.

'He obviously enjoyed it,' she thought.

So she was unprepared the next morning when she woke him and he said, 'But I went yesterday. I don't need to go anymore do I?'

'I am afraid so Peter you have to go every day Monday to Friday like Anne does,' she told him.

'But I want to stay home with you and Sarah,' he beseeched her.

'I am sorry Peter, but you must get up and get dressed, there's a good boy.' She went downstairs. She could hear him crying, but what more could she say. She needed him to be at school. With Sarah taking up quite a bit of her time she needed all the spare time for her work as well as taking bookings for the hire firm. They had needed to have a phone installed, which was an added expense, but necessary. Things had been better between herself and Gary, he liked being his own boss, he said it made him feel important.

It was not long before Gary had to take on another driver. They were getting long distance journeys, to the airports, as well as covering local taxi journeys. The wedding hire business was also growing, and she had taken on a young girl to help her. People came from far and wide, and their accountant kept telling her that she was still making far more money than Gary, but she kept this information to herself. He believed he was doing well, but unfortunately his overheads were high. Wages and car maintenance and petrol absorbed a lot of their profits.

The taxi hire continued to grow, and within a year there were three full time drivers and two part time drivers at weekends to cover weddings. They had bought a further car, a large black Humber Pullman to be used for the brides, and rented another two black Ford Zodiacs. With so many cars, Gary had asked his friend Bill to work part time for them as a car mechanic. This kept the cars on the road, and saved garage bills. It was at this time that the local Council decided to licence taxis, and the drivers had to pass a test and become hackney carriage drivers. The licences for the cars were expensive, but every car had to have a hackney plate attached to the back of it. They had also rented a stand in the town centre, and the rent was exorbitant, but gave them lots of work, which was good because this paid the drivers wages.

She learnt to drive a car, a nice little man called Mr Pendleton took her out each week in an Austin A40 car and taught her the rudiments of driving. She had quite a few lessons, before he felt she was ready to take her driving test. The nearest test centre was at Newbury, a town she did not know very well. she failed her first test, she had been so nervous. Her second test was not much better, and she was beginning to think she would never pass. Her third attempt however was successful, and she was delighted when the examiner told her she had passed. Gary had been chiding her for the past week that she would never pass, and kept laughing at her.

Over the next two years, the money flowed, but time and again the accountant reiterated that the car hire business was making a loss, and suggesting they close it. But Margaret knew she had to keep Gary employed, and believing he was earning good money, this kept their relationship going. She loved Gary, but she knew deep down that they were not happy, she certainly wasn't. Her life was filled with work and her family to care for. It would do, but there was no romance, no joy in her life. There were times she looked at Gary and wished he were Sandy. Her mother had been right, she had made a terrible mistake.

Still there was no point crying over spilt milk, she had responsibilities. She suggested to Gary that they should take some time out for themselves, and having found a lady willing to sit in with the children for a few hours once a fortnight, they started going out for a meal at a Bernie Inn a few miles away. Margaret made herself a couple of long dresses, and wore them on these evenings, and Gary put on his best suit. It was reasonably enjoyable, although they had little to talk about except the children, if they talked about the business, they often argued. Gary wanted to continue to expand, but Margaret felt they should curb expenditure and appreciate what they had. These evenings usually ended with them returning home, and Gary taking her upstairs and making love to her, or that is what he called it. Unfortunately although Margaret needed to feel his arms around her, he never told her he loved her, and her needs were never met. She often lay in bed for hours, often crying, wishing for things to be different. He seemed content, perhaps it was just her that was being silly she thought. But she knew there was more to life and love than this. But she felt so desolate.

He didn't understand her, and she did not understand herself.

*****

She had an idea, she had saved some money, and suggested to Gary that they could afford a week's holiday during the school summer holidays. Everything seemed quite expensive until she saw an advertisement for a week's holiday in Calella, Spain, for £25 per adult all in and half price for the children. This would include the flight and their holiday hotel. There would be little spending money, but she could just manage this. They had never flown to Spain before, but she was sure the children would enjoy it, although Margaret was not keen on the idea of flying in an aeroplane.

She was pleased that Gary actually agreed, and straightaway he started boasting to everyone that he was off to Spain. She knew he was always fascinated with aircraft, and no doubt he would look forward to the journey. The children were thrilled and Margaret took the opportunity to point out to Gary how useful her income was. He made little comment, but she was pleased that both he and the children enjoyed the week away. He had been so kind and thoughtful, and she really felt it had been worth the sacrifice of the money she had saved, which she should have used to pay up the building society. It had been lovely with lots of warm sunshine. The beach however, had been shingle and not very pleasant to sit on. Even sitting on their towels did not detract from the hard lumpy shingle.

One day at the hotel Anne and Peter had been sent upstairs to their room to wash their hands before dinner. They came back having intimated that they had washed them.

During the course of dinner Margaret noticed that the staff were rushing round and shouting, and because she did not understand the language she could not decide what was going on. It was not until they all went upstairs to their rooms that she realised the commotion was all along their landing. That the door to Anne and Peter's room was open and water was everywhere. The staff were mopping up.

She later learnt from the courier that the hotel water tanks had emptied, and presumably when the children had gone to wash their hands, they had put the taps on, and the plug in the sink, but no water had come out of the taps, they had left it.

While they were having dinner, the water tanks had been refilled, and the sink had soon filled and overflowed, flooding everything. It took a day or two for the pandemonium to die down, and people to stop staring at them all around the hotel. But all in all the holiday was a success. Gary appeared grateful for the holiday, and Margaret decided she could cope with anything. Perhaps the holiday would change things.

In 1967 just before Christmas, she started to feel terribly unwell. She went to see her doctor who told her she had flu, and to go home and stay in bed for a couple of days. She went home, but with the children and a big wedding dress order, she could not go to bed. She struggled on, and some three weeks later she went back to the doctor again who once more examined her. 'Well Mrs Pearce, you will be pleased to learn you are pregnant,' he told her.

'*Pregnant*, I can't be,' she looked dumbfounded at the doctor.

'I can assure you Mrs Pearce you are and I am sorry it is stressful to you. 'I am sure you will absorb the shock and things will sort themselves out,' he said.

Margaret drove home feeling desolate and that evening she told Gary. He blazed at her. 'It can't be mine, have you been seeing one of the drivers when I was not here?' he screamed at her. 'Who is it?' he questioned her.

'Gary I have not been with anyone except you, please believe me.' She replied. He got up from his chair and hit her. 'I bet, you even look guilty.' He shouted at her.

Tears poured down her face. How could she convince him, and also that she felt so unwell. She ran out of the house and down the road. He did not follow her, she walked for what seemed ages. What could she do, how could he be so horrible to her?

Of course she hadn't been with anyone else, what was he thinking of? It was over an hour later that she returned to the house. A more subdued Gary came to meet her. 'I am sorry. I didn't mean to go on at you, it will be all right, I cannot understand what is wrong with me. I think it is because my father never trusted my mother, and with good reason. Two of my brothers do not belong to my father, so perhaps that is why I react like this, I am sorry Margaret.'

It made her feel a little better, but not much, she just wanted him to put his arms around her, and promise her his love but that was not to be. It was as if the person she had been on holiday with did not exist anymore.

Now she would have to work really hard for a few months as in the past she knew things would get worse nearer the time of the birth, and she would have to give up for a time. Things were not good financially, but they were going to get ten times worse.

CHAPTER 11

It was no wonder the doctor had firstly thought she had 'flu', every day she felt very unwell, but she soldiered on with the dresses she had on order, as well as taking charge of the new mobile control system which Gary had insisted they needed to be up to date ensuring that taxi journeys were attended to immediately thus keeping abreast of the competition in the town They were unable to pay someone to work the system, so she had the job.

What with answering the telephone and keeping in touch with the drivers, she found less and less time to sew. This meant that she had to stay up well into the night to complete the orders she had on hand. She constantly felt very tired, but Gary now seemed to have turned over a new leaf and when she finally got to bed, made love to her. Of course she could not get pregnant again at present, so it was an admirable opportunity for him to have his conjugal rights. Margaret needed his closeness, it sustained her through the long days, what with the school journeys, preparing meals and sorting out the wages for the drivers, she was kept very busy.

They had no social life, except for her mother's visits, and John and Elsa coming over from Reading from time to time. John enjoyed playing her piano, as he did not have one anymore, and sometimes they would play a duet together. Gary liked visiting his mother who still lived in Ham, and to see his brothers. Margaret did not enjoy the journey there and back very much, because Gary had taken to driving much faster, and she became frightened. He just laughed at her.

So life revolved very much around work and the children. The winter months drew to a close, and Margaret derived a lot of pleasure from the spring weather. She sowed some vegetables in the garden, and took a bit of time out to sew some dresses for the girls, both Anne and Sarah had very little in the way of dresses which they would need for the coming summer months.

Gary was always watching her with the drivers. He started to become obsessed with the idea she was encouraging them to stay and talk with her at the house. He would call over the tannoy system asking where Jack or Bill were. He could mostly know where they were if they were on the road working, but on one occasion Jack had stayed to talk to her about his wife, and what he could do to sort out a particular problem. She had sat talking with him for some twenty minutes, when all of a sudden Gary arrived at the house and wanted to know what Jack was still doing there, when there were taxi journeys to do.

Jack jumped up and apologised, saying he had got carried away with his problems. But Gary was furious, and after he had left accused her to keeping him there. 'What was he really after?' he accused her.

'Nothing Gary, he was just talking about his wife,' she replied. She could feel him trembling with rage 'He is having problems with his wife, that is all,' she continued.

'A likely tale, more like he was trying to get off with you,' he shouted at her. He just had not wanted to see reason, and she was glad when she had to go out and collect the children from school. Dinner that night was a very silent affair. Gary was not talking to her, and if he wanted anything from her he asked one of the children to ask her. How childlike she thought. He sulked for two or three days.

Her belly was growing rapidly in size, and she wondered whether she could be having twins, but the midwife had reassured her on her last antenatal clinic appointment that there was only one child inside her.

She completed a large order for a wedding dress and six bridesmaids dresses. The money certainly came in useful, but although they managed to pay their staff and pay most of the bills, the mortgage once more started to fall into arrears. It didn't matter what she did, she could not stop it.

She became the size of a whale over the next few months, and at the beginning of July, she started to have back pain. She had already stopped sewing, there was no way she could get down on the floor and pin hems, so she rested as much as she could. By the 12th of the month, and being overdue by a week, she took some caster oil with orange juice, trying to induce the labour. Within a day she had succeeded, and on a very hot day she gave birth to another baby girl. Gary had stayed with her for the birth. It was the only baby she had delivered at home. the midwife had kept him busy boiling water and making tea. So it was with some relief when the baby finally made her appearance into the world.

Margaret held the child in her arms, and said to Gary, 'I don't know what to call her, I only had a name for a boy ready.'

'Well I don't know,' he relied. 'Let us ask the children.'

The children had apparently been sitting on the stairs whilst the baby was being born. Gary opened the door of the bedroom, and they all trooped in to see their new sister, they all stared in wonder at the baby wrapped in a soft white woollen shawl.

'We do not know what to call her, any ideas?' she asked them. The children thought for a while, and then Anne decided that Katy sounded a nice name. So Katy it was.

Katy was a real disruption to the house, and never appeared to stop crying. Anne would often take her for a walk out in the pram to give their mother a rest.

Mrs Trent was delighted that she had yet another granddaughter and quickly made herself indispensable, and would get Gary to pick her up and come over to help. Helping meant just looking after Katy, but it did leave Margaret free to go back to making dresses again, as well as keeping everything else ticking over.

The accountant once more chided her on the folly of keeping the taxi side going. 'It looks fine on paper, but in practical terms you are running at a loss,' he told her. She knew, but was fearful of the consequences. Gary would be out of work.

Within a year, she knew things were coming to a head. Although she worked very hard and hired out lots of dresses, and made so many she could not make the figures work.

They were offered a contract for school journeys, to the local Preparatory School, where pupils paid to attend, and she took this on board herself, and tied it in with taking her children to school. The headteacher told her that they needed a teacher for needlework and craft urgently, so she arranged to go once a week to teach needlework. She had had no formal training, but was very skilled. A few weeks later she discovered that they needed a teacher for religious instruction. She did have her theology certificate and she had organised the Sunday school lessons at Ham Church, so she offered to take that on board as well.

Gary complained she was often away from the house, and asked her who was going to take on the running of the office and answer the telephone. She suggested that he could do that for the few times she was away from the house. 'I have driving commitments, I cannot be in two places at once,' he shouted at her. He would not listen to reason, but she persevered, leaving the office unmanned twice a week for an hour a time. It could not be helped.

The building society were continually writing to them, demanding payment of the arrears, with warning notices, which worried her. She started to look for another house which might be suitable, so they could use some of their equity and sort things out, but the price of houses was rising and anything suitable they could not afford.

In desperation she went to see Ted, but he could not help her. What was she to do? She hardly slept at night, what with working until two or three o'clock and then tossing and turning, she became exhausted, and it was not long before she became ill with a bad case of gastric 'flu' which left her terribly tired and depressed. She could see no way out of the situation until the beginning of 1970.

CHAPTER 12

At the beginning of 1970 Margaret was aware that things were going from bad to worse and that money was in short supply. She started to scan the local papers for a full time job. The children were growing fast, and although she still had her youngest daughter on her hands, who was almost two years old, she knew she had to earn some regular money. The talents that she possessed could not support her anymore. She had spent many years dressmaking, and teaching part time at schools in the local area, a few hours a week. But she needed something more permanent, and always in the back of her mind, was the idea that she wanted to work helping other people, especially children.

At the end of January she saw an advertisement for an Education Welfare Officer in the local area, which would entail visiting schools and families to do with the welfare of children. It looked interesting although she had no clear idea of what the job would actually entail. She decided to apply. *Nothing ventured - nothing gained* she thought, and sent off for an application form. When it arrived, she read the job description two or three times. '*I could do that*' was her first thought. Suddenly she felt quite excited, a job working with children, and she could work from home. Surely Gary her husband would approve.

Gary was a very possessive man, and was not in favour of his wife going out to work. He preferred her to be at home looking after his creature comforts and that of the children. But the wage he brought home was not enough, especially with the cost of the new addition to the family. As soon as he came home from work she showed him the advertisement.

'It's a full time job,' he cried.'

'Yes I know,' Margaret replied, 'but I can work from home and take the children to and from school, and I will be home by 5pm each day, I am sure I could manage this job, Gary.' But he was quite adamant she should not apply.

She put the advertisement away, and decided he might be right, it was a lot of hours, and she would have to do escort duty to various parts of the country from time to time. The doubts continued. A week later she was about to throw out the old newspaper when she saw the advertisement staring out of the newspaper at her. '*I must apply*,' she thought, '*it is too good an opportunity to miss.*' She studied it carefully then without a moment's hesitation, she sent the application form. Having done so, she also felt positive that she had little chance of getting the post, after all she had never done anything like it before.

Two weeks went by and she forgot all about it. She was busy at the Tavistock school getting ready for the Easter Holidays. She was also very busy running the home. Her children always had need of her and the toddler took up a lot of her time, although Anne her eldest daughter helped her a lot.

She was not prepared for the letter arriving from the Education Department, with a date set for an interview at Winchester some two weeks hence. She rang to confirm she would attend. The lady she spoke to told her she would be one of the first ladies applying for the post. Apparently the job had always been given to a man in the past. This really unnerved her.

She knew she was probably out of her depth, but nothing would deter her from going to the interview. Gary just laughed when she told him it was a job for a man, 'You are wasting your time,' he told her, but he was also confident she would not get the job. Her rebellious instinct came to the fore, 'I'm going.'

Two weeks later she drove to Winchester. She wore her one and only suit. It was navy blue and hugged her slim figure. She had decided to wear a crisp white blouse and her favourite pearl earrings. It was a cold, spring day. The sky had been heavy and threatened rain. She drove slowly south along the A30 toward her destination in Winchester, mulling over the possible questions she would be asked about her background.

She was so nervous she could hardly stop shaking, as she made her way to the Education Office. All the candidates had been shown into a waiting room on the first floor. There were three men in the room when she arrived. No other women.

'*I must be mad,*' she thought, they had told her the post nearly always went to a man. Perhaps Gary was right.

The first man was called in. He had a briefcase tucked under his arm. Twenty minutes later he came out and announced to one of the other applicants he had had a marvellous interview and gave the impression he had secured the job. Each one in turn went in. Then she heard her name called. With her heart in her mouth she was taken into a room where two men sat behind a large desk. Each stood and shook her hand. She sat down on the lonely chair which had been placed facing them. The questions started. '*I shall be glad when it's all over,*' she thought, '*go home to Gary who will say, 'I told you so'.*'

The two men interviewing her were so pleasant she gradually relaxed. They told her she could break for lunch. The interview had lasted forty minutes. They might just have well have said go home she thought. She left the building and wandered down into the town, but was too nervous to eat. She finally drank a cup of tea in a café, and returned to the waiting room and sat reading a book she had found on a table, all about the beginning of the BBC. She was quite engrossed even though the other candidates had come back and were talking to each other, with rather pompous voices, and ignoring her. It made her jump when her name was called. She sprang up and followed the rather prim woman down the corridor to the interview room once more.

'Here we go,' she thought, *'they will now tell me 'we are sorry to inform you'.'* As she went in the door, both men stood up, then smiled warmly and asked her to sit down. One of them had a piece of paper in his hand. 'Mrs Pearce we are pleased to offer you the post of Education Welfare Officer,' the bald headed man said. He had a very kind face and smiled warmly at Margaret. She could not for the life of her remember his name, although he had introduced himself to her earlier in the day. She had been so nervous, all she had been able to think about then was how soon she could go home.

'We were both most impressed with your answers and feel you will be the most suitable person for the job. Not only do we feel your personality is just right for the job, but you would be bringing a wealth of knowledge of family life with you.' He went on, 'You will be one of the first women we have appointed to this post. It is felt that women may well offer a different style and image to the profession, at present many people look on the Education Welfare Officer at the School Board Man.'

She was dumbstruck. How she managed to smile and shake hands, she never knew, as well as agreeing to take the job. She left the building floating on air. And what about those three very eminent gentlemen who had also been interviewed? She mused about this as she drove home. The nearer she came to her home town the more she wondered if she had done the right thing. Could she manage the job, the house and the children, especially when they were ill. What would Gary say now! One thing was for sure he would not be pleased, even though she was going to earn over £1000 a year. She could afford to give up the dressmaking, which caused her terrible eye strain.

******

In April 1970 she started work as an Education Welfare Officer. She firstly went to Winchester to talk with the bald headed man, who she now knew was Michael Lambert, and was the Senior Manager of the Education Department. Apparently, it was to him that she would answer for any decisions she made in the course of her work.

'Do sit down, Mrs Pearce. Firstly I will show you all the forms that the department uses, some of which I will give you to take away, and keep at your home, which you will use as your office.' There were forms for non school attendance, uniform grants, free school meals for children whose parents could ill afford them, legal forms when applying to the court for Supervision Orders, or Care Orders in respect of children, headed paper and a stack of envelopes. She spent the entire first day being introduced to staff members working in the department, who she would contact if she had a problem. At 4 o'clock she was sent home, just in time to collect Katy from her mother's before cooking the evening meal. Anne had been extremely good, and had laid the table and was minding the children. Margaret really appreciated her eldest daughter.

Anne was a good girl, and currently attending one of the local comprehensive schools. She was fourteen years of age, a pretty girl who was very popular with all her friends. Over the last eighteen months Anne had helped her mother with little Katy. The child was very attention-seeking and demanding and cried a lot, and usually got what she wanted. Anne spoilt her and so did her son Peter. Sarah her middle daughter was a very quiet child, and usually kept to her own devices. She was very intelligent and read a lot of books, and studied hard. She was quite happy completing homework set for her by her school. She attended the local Junior school, but outshone all of her classmates.

They were all so different. Peter hated school, and could not wait to get home, and out with his friends. He was due to start at Anne's comprehensive school that September. He would far rather stay home and help the mechanic who looked after his father's cars. Although Anne was a good girl in the main, she often taunted Peter, and a lot of the time they had fights about all sorts of things.

One day she was up in her bedroom, playing her recorder. Peter flung open her bedroom door and demanded she stop the noise; she continued to play it. He raced across the floor, and wrestled with her trying to take the recorder away from her. Margaret could hear them shouting at each other, but took little notice, deciding it would all get sorted out. The next thing she heard was a loud bang and the sound of glass breaking.

She raced upstairs where they both stood staring at the windowpane which was clearly broken. 'What on earth are you two doing?' she demanded. Anne turned to her mother and told her that they had been fighting over her recorder and the mouthpiece had come off and smashed into the window.

Margaret felt fear clutch her heart. Gary would be home soon. What would he say, she thought. She turned to Peter, 'You had better go down and clear up the glass before someone has an accident, I don't want the dog having a cut paw.' Peter went off to do her bidding.

She made the two children apologise to each other, but warned them that their father would be home shortly.

Margaret continued to prepare the dinner but her mind was on the broken window.

When Gary came home he was not in a very good mood, and he soon learnt about the window from Sarah. Gary charged up the stairs and looked at the damage. He then shouted for Peter to go upstairs. It was like watching a lamb go to the slaughter. You could see the fear on Peter's face as he climbed the stairs.

Margaret could hear him shouting at the child and the next minute she heard Peter cry out as his father hit him again and again.

She was terrified of Gary when he was in a rage but was concerned with Peter's dilemma. She ran up the stairs, Peter's bedroom door was open, she could see blood running down the boy's face. She shouted to Gary to stop. He turned and came toward her. 'Do you want some?' He raised his hand to strike her.

She took a step backwards fearful she would fall down the steep stairs. The interruption however worked. Gary turned and continued to shout at the child but did not hit him anymore. She returned to the kitchen, tears flowed down her face. How she hated Gary when he hurt Peter. It did not seem to matter who was in the wrong. Peter always got the blame and was punished often for things he never did. Peter could do nothing right in his father's eyes, however hard he tried. He would punish him by sending him to bed with no dinner or worse follow him up the stairs and terrorise the boy by hitting and shouting at him. Gary came down the stairs, his face blood red with temper, and shouted, 'Peter is grounded for a week.' Margaret's heart was heavy, what could she do, she knew he should never have hit Peter like he had. She served up Gary's dinner and then went upstairs and bathed Peter's nose, washing away the blood.

She promised him she would be up later and take him some dinner.

After dinner, Anne came into the kitchen and said she would take up Peter's dinner. Margaret could see she felt guilty about the whole incident, after all it was mainly her fault it had happened. What a terrible day. Where was the loving , caring person she thought she had married. She was sure Gary still believed Peter was not his child and took it out on him, though anyone could see the strong likeness of father and son.

As the months went by she realised things were getting out of control. She had so much to do, what with looking after the family, and working so many hours a day, as well as studying, her natural strength deteriorated. Margaret's health started to show a weakness, and she developed IBS, some days she felt fine others she felt dreadful. Her doctor put her on hormone tablets which seemed to help but the problem never went away.

******

Gary her husband still had his own business, hiring cars and driving private hire cars, taking people to the airports or the local railway station, but the business was not doing very well. All their money seemed to go towards the upkeep of the cars, or for paying the part time drivers. It had been a struggle for some time. As predicted Gary was not pleased that Margaret had secured a full time job, and even less so when he learnt that one of the Education Welfare Officers from the Winchester area, had been asked to come up to Harmsworth and be with her during her first week, showing her what to do, and advising her how to use all the forms she had been given. Over a cup of tea at her house he told her roughly what the job entailed. Arnold was a nice guy in his late fifties, and he told her he had been doing the job for years. She had to visit schools in the area, and check on children's attendance. The children who were off school for no given reason, warranted a visit to their homes to see why they were away. Some parents would forget to advise the school why their child was absent, but many were children playing truant.

Arnold told her of some of the places children frequented when not attending school. They often headed for the town centre, the local parks if the weather was good, if not local cafés, the shopping arcades, the local cinema or their friends houses to name a few. It would be her job to ensure these children returned to school, and to advise their parents that the child had been truanting.

Then there were the children kept at home to do child minding of their siblings whilst their parents were absent, either working or going out for the day. He stressed that he worried about children who were working illegally, sometimes in the local market, but more especially children working on the land, driving tractors or using chainsaws. He told her that one of her tasks was to control the employment of children under a certain age and to issue employment cards to children working legally, delivering newspapers each day before school and those working on a Saturday, part time in the local shops. Margaret felt sure she could cope with that. She enjoyed a little detective work, though she was not sure about taking the children or their parents to court for not attending school. She had no training and felt that she knew very little about the law.

Arnold told her it was easy, and showed her the forms she would need to complete and take along to the Clerk of the local court. She felt very nervous about this part of the job but he assured her he would come up the first time she went to court and 'hold her hand'. 'I suggest you change your name from Margaret to Maggie, it sounds more friendly, and more you.' He smiled at her.

'I think I like the sound of that,' she replied.

She soon learnt that the school visiting entailed listening to school teachers concerned about their pupils behaviour, especially if they were likely to be excluded from school, and also the children who appeared to have problems stemming from their home life. lack of school uniforms, not having money for school outings or insufficient money for school dinners. Mr Lambert at Winchester had primed her about the allowances provided by the Government towards pupil welfare.

Then there were the local special schools for children who were deaf or had a disability, such as a mental handicap. But many children were despatched to special schools many miles away, and having to leave their families for a term or half a term at a time. Margaret found she had to escort many children to other towns all over the country, because of social or behavioural problems. She found it very sad when the children were collected from home, as they often cried, not wanting to leave their mothers, and she had to cheer them up on the journey. She learnt the knack of persuading them it was just a few weeks at a time they would be away, and playing games with them as they went along such as 'I spy' or 'Looking for funny car registration number plates'. Sometimes she would have them singing jolly songs or a round of spelling B.

All this she gradually fitted into her working week. She was determined to make a success of this job but then there was the family - her family which had great need of her, and some days she felt very tired.

It was very hard at first, but soon it all slipped into a daily routine. Gary was usually up first, and off driving before 8am. She eased herself out of bed about 7am and raced round encouraging the children to get up and dressed. Once breakfast was over she took the three elder children to school and then took Katy to her mother's before starting on her planned day. Her daily visits to the schools took priority before she visited the children's parents, unfortunately many of them both worked during the day and more and more she found she had to visit in the evening. This meant putting her children to bed and then going out again. Gary was livid. 'You are always working,' he would say.

'I know,' she replied, 'but it is the only way to see some of the parents, can't you understand?'

Gary's jealous streak showed itself time and again and he continually chided her that she was seeing someone else. She knew this was preposterous but he kept on and on about it. To put things in perspective because she worked some hours in the evening, she was able to have a few hours at home in the daytime (usually a long lunch hour) when she could get things done in the house. There was always stacks of ironing with a large family, and trying hard to keep things clean and tidy. After just a few weeks, knowing that she would be earning quite a lot of money each month she decided that she would try and find a woman prepared to come in and do some of the housework two mornings a week. She felt this would be a real help, and would also relieve some of the tasks she set Anne to do.

Margaret learnt from her mother that her sister May was moving to Harmsworth, from London, and would be living close within a mile of their house. It seemed everyone was moving near to them.

CHAPTER 13

The town of Harmsworth was originally a small country market town, but over the years it had grown taking in quite a lot of people known as the London Overspill. The town had been divided into two sections by the Education Department. Margaret covered the southern half and just recently a young man had been appointed to the northern area. Tom Banks was a very likeable young man. Margaret learnt that he was in his mid thirties and single. He was living in lodgings in a small village just outside the town. His landlady was an elderly widow, and did not like him having visitors, so when it was necessary for him to discuss anything with her he always came to her house. She found him very easy to get on with and if she found it difficult to do an escort duty, he would often volunteer to do it for her. In return she often invited him to stay to dinner. He was always grateful for a good meal and he got on well with the children.

Gary took every opportunity to chide her about Tom. He disliked it that Tom came to the house when he himself was out working, and many a time accused Margaret of having an affair with him. She always retaliated, pointing out her home was also her office. 'I suppose he told you to change your name to Maggie,' he threw at her. She would not be drawn.

Tom had a girlfriend called Jenny and he often talked to Margaret about her, and told her he hoped to marry Jenny one day, but not until he had saved up enough money to buy a house, possibly in Devon where houses were cheaper. He envisaged transferring to that area doing the same job.

The months rolled by. Arnold came up from Winchester when she took her first child to court for non attendance and she was jubilant when the magistrate ordered a Supervision Order to be placed on the child for one year. The boy who was eleven years old was also warned that if he did not go to school his parents could be fined a lot of money, or it would be considered whether he should be sent away to a special boarding school. This case was the first of many, but Margaret preferred to persuade children to go to school, rather than take them to court.

She loved the school holidays. The schools themselves were closed, but her time was occupied by delivering school uniform grants or filling up forms for parents to apply for free school meals. Working from home had its benefits, she was able to mind her own children during school holidays, and pop in and out when necessary. There was always a lot of paperwork, which had to be despatched to Winchester, and it took up a lot of her time, notwithstanding composing court reports.

One day she had to call on a Mr Turner in Woods Road, regarding school uniform grants for his two daughters. When she drew up outside the house, she found him up a ladder painting the outside of the house. Knowing he was on sick benefit for a bad back she was surprised. He came down and took her inside the house, where she discovered that his wife was again pregnant. He saw the look on her face, and confirmed that his back was still too bad to go to work. She felt he was claiming fraudulently, but said nothing.

During conversation on this visit, and on subsequent visits to this house, she learnt a lot of information from him on how the 'system' worked and what you could claim for. He was a very nice man but she gradually learnt he was rather work shy, and he knew all his rights.

It had taken a while but she had finally found a woman to help clean the house. She fitted in so well. Joan was about fifty years of age and had a lot of spare time on her hands. Her husband was always down working on his allotment and there were just the two of them at home. She often helped out with a bit of child minding as well. Gary quite liked her, even though he had opposed Margaret taking someone on to do her job caring for the family. Joan spoilt him and he revelled in the attention she gave him.

Two years went by before the first hiccup occurred. A letter arrived from Mr Lambert, asking Margaret to go to Winchester, as he needed to talk to her. Her first reaction was to think she had done something wrong and she worried about this for days.

It was a warm sunny day in June when she drove down to the County Town. Feeling apprehensive she entered the Education Offices and reported to Mr Lambert's secretary; who advised her he was expecting her. Within minutes he came out of his office and walked towards her extending his hand and smiling most profusely. 'How nice to see you Mrs Pearce, do come in and make yourself comfortable.' She followed him into his office and sat down. 'You are probably wondering what I wanted to see you about,' he said. She nodded. 'Well I must tell you firstly, that we are very pleased with your progress. You have accomplished a great deal in the Harmsworth area and we feel it would be to your advantage for us to send you on a course to become a qualified Education Welfare Officer. How do you feel about that?' Margaret did not know what to say. She was happy they were pleased with her work, but to go on a course, her mind raced.

'Can you tell me what that would entail Mr Lambert?' she asked.

'It would mean the department would sponsor you on a day release basis to a college in Southampton, one day a week, I believe it is a Friday. We would pay all your expenses and the course would last two years. In that time you would study the work of Central Government, Local Government and the Social Services. The course also encompasses Child Welfare, English and elements of Psychology.' All the things she had wanted to study at Grammar School and had not had the opportunity.

What he was saying convinced Margaret that it was possible for her to do this. She would work four days a week as normal in her area, and on a Friday would attend college, with all expenses paid. 'I think I would like to try that,' she said, 'I would obviously have to talk to my husband about it, but I am sure there will not be a problem.'

'Wonderful,' he moved some papers on his desk and then said, 'Once you have qualified, you will get an extra salary rise, on top of your annual one.'

Margaret thought, well Gary will approve of extra money, there should not be a problem. She thanked Mr Lambert and shook hands with him before departing back to Harmsworth.

Thing were going well. The house was running smoothly, the children were well, and Gary got on well with Joan. She returned home as happy as can be. The only fly in the ointment was the eviction notice they had received earlier that week, but she would talk to the building society about that.

Her happy mood was soon to be changed, for when Gary came home and she told him what Mr Lambert had offered, he flew into a rage, demanding to know what she was thinking about, and what about her family, and him especially. Who was going to look after him?

'Gary it will just be a working day like any other, and everything is running smoothly, everyone is catered for. I would just be home a little later on a Friday, as I would have to drive back from Southampton,' she cried. Gary went out and slammed the door, and he continued to sulk for a further two days. Everyone in the house talked in whispers not daring to speak out loud.

It was a week before things returned to normal. Gary gradually came round and after a lot of discussion agreed she could go.

She was very busy with lots of home visits to do. One of these visits had concerned a family who had seventeen children. They all lived in a large council house, where the local council had given them two semi detached houses, and knocked through a door between the two, so that they had six bedrooms and two bathrooms altogether. Margaret called to see Mrs Chillery because she often kept one or other of the children home to help her and look after the others if they were ill. She soon learnt the best time to find the family at home was on any wet afternoon, when it was raining. Mr Chillery was a painter and decorator, and when it rained he stayed home, and when she called, he would appear at the bedroom window, both he and his wife would be in bed. He would come down and let her in saying he and the Mrs were resting.

It was often hard to encourage parents like these that school work was important, quite often because they themselves had missed out on education, their argument being that children could learn a trade, and that academic work was a waste of time. But she had persisted and would take any child at home into school.

It took a little extra organisation to arrange that everything continued so that there were no recriminations from Gary, whilst she set about the task of learning the skills needed for her to be a good Welfare Officer. She looked forward to Friday from the moment she started the course in the September. It was a tremendous strain, attending lectures at the college and also studying at home besides working four days a week at her job, which she did not want to suffer. Along with many of the colleagues she had come to know quite well, from the many meetings she had attended at Winchester, she spent her day soaking up every bit of information she could, as well as using the college library, and borrowing lots of books to glean the answers to questions set by the tutors.

Margaret suddenly started to blossom, and much of this was to do with the camaraderie she shared with the other students. They were all great characters. There was Ben who was so very popular because of his great sense of humour, which had the whole class in fits of laughter at times, and Bob who never agreed with the tutor, causing ructions, and great debates took place about controversial issues.

Margaret had become very friendly with Andrea who lived at Wickham. They often had lunch together in the refectory or would wander into the local town for lunch as well as a little shopping spree. Andrea had a lovely natural ability to bemoan anything or anyone, which touched her own sense of humour. She partly looked forward to Fridays just to sit with Andrea and chat. She was also able to offload some of her worries about coping, and how Gary did not like her attending and was very much against her proving she should be allowed to go on and apply for another course which was being suggested that the students consider to follow on from this one where she would then qualify as a Social Worker.

'I should not worry if I were you, I am sure he will be delighted if you pass these exams, and would surely allow you the chance to progress,' Andrea said. But Margaret knew only too well how Gary ticked, and if he knew she had to go away for a year from home for the final year he would never allow it.

The tutors were quick to assess everyone's skills and as she had originally thought they felt she was good at both communications and working with children.

At home one evening she said to Gary, 'I know this is what I want to do, and I am enjoying this present course tremendously.' Gary was becoming more and more adamant that she should give it up. His negative views grated on her. *'Why can't he encourage me?'* she thought, *'after all I am already doing the job, and it would be nice to be qualified.'*

Her departmental manager Mr Hughes was supportive and he often reassured her that when she passed, firstly her salary would rise, which would be wonderful, and secondly she would have the equivalent status of an Intermediate Graduate.

Two other ladies on the course, Jenny and Dawn, were to become very good friends. There were twenty four members of the class altogether, although she never came to know all of them as well as her immediate friends. It was fun to go to lunch with her friends and make a break from her home life.

The course consisted of lectures in six subjects. She studied Local Government, and learnt all about County Councils and District Councils. Then she studied Central Government, which related to how the laws of the land were passed in London, under the heading Social Policy. As a child she had detested learning about history, mainly because of the teacher who had taught her. That teacher had been unable to control the class very well, and the subject had always been boring. But learning Constitutional History now with her colleagues she found it fascinating; especially when the Speaker of the House of Commons Sir Horace King came and gave a lecture. What a knowledgeable man he was and so interesting.

Childcare came as second nature to her. This consisted of learning Human Growth and Development of children. And then learning about how the Social Services of the country operated. This gave her an insight into what she felt was the culmination of what she wanted to do. How she would love to go on and train as a Social Worker.

The sixth subject was English. She had always been good at English when she was at school, albeit a long time ago. She found it was a great deal of help when she was composing her court reports as well as the many essays she had to complete.

Two months into the course, the students were all taken to London to visit the Houses of Parliament. Margaret went up on the train, and met her colleagues outside the awe inspiring building. There were hundreds of people milling round the entrance, but quite quickly they were chaperoned into the entrance of the House of Lords by a guide. As they followed him up the grand staircase and through the gallery he kept up a constant stream of information. How the Queen opened Parliament each year, usually in the late autumn - The State Opening of Parliament - they were shown the robing room and followed through the galleries to the chamber itself. Margaret was not prepared for the intense beauty of it. The red and gold. It was beautiful, like nothing she had ever seen before. Of course Ben, in his usual manner decided to leave the group, and went and sat on the Woolsack. The guide was not amused, and Ben was promptly told to rejoin the group. Margaret could envisage the Queen sitting on the throne in her regal robes, which overlooked the chamber.

Their group moved on through the vast building, until they were outside the House of Commons. They were all encouraged to rub the foot of Winston Churchill's statue, before entering the other chamber. How totally different it was. It was brown, with green leather benches. The guide told them that the very tall chair, placed in the middle at one end was always occupied by the Speaker of the House of Commons, currently Sir Horace king who had come to the college just a few weeks before, and from whom they had learnt so much. Margaret could almost sense the debates which took place here, and was overjoyed when the guide told them that Sir Horace had made arrangements for anyone who wished to listen to a debate, could do so, by attending the Strangers Gallery that afternoon.

They all disbanded at lunch time, but Margaret decided that she would like to listen to a debate. So she had some lunch in a little restaurant, frequented by the MPs just across the road. It was quite expensive and Gary would have been shocked to learn of her extravagance, but she thought, it is just a one-off, not that she would ever have told him.

Andrea had decided to stay with her, and also Ben. They made their way to the Strangers Gallery at 2pm as instructed, and took their seats, which were right at the front. Margaret could see everything, and soon the MPs filed in and took their seats on the benches. There was a lot of chattering, until a man called the house to order on the arrival of The Speaker. Margaret was thrilled, to think she had sat right by him when he had come to the college. She almost felt she knew him or he knew her. The first debate began. A member stood up and started to raise a question, and then various other members replied. Voices became raised, and Ben whispered that it was like watching children squabble. Margaret didn't agree but just smiled at him. All too soon it was time to leave and catch the train back to Hampshire.

The first year at college came to an end. Margaret was able to stop doing the ironing with a book she was studying in her other hand. The essays were all finished, and a date had been set for everyone to sit the first of six examinations.

There was nothing further to do, and she returned to her job full time. She knew that if she failed any of the three examinations she was to sit, she should fail them all, and have to take them again, as well as the three subjects she would be studying the following year at College.

She became embroiled once more in her job and made lots of home visits during the next few weeks. She was very concerned about a lady called Mrs Kendrick, who was married to an alcoholic, who often hit her. She had been asked to call on the family by the year head at the local comprehensive school. Mr and Mrs Kendrick had two children, Simon who was 11 years old and in the first year, and his younger sister who was 9 who attended the local junior school. Simon was not doing very well with his school work, and in conversation with his year head he had indicated that he was afraid for his mother, especially when his father had been drinking heavily, or he had lost money on the horses.

Margaret had learnt that Mrs Kendrick was afraid of her husband and wanted to leave him but did not know how to go about it. Margaret suggested to her she should see a solicitor. Mrs Kendrick was fearful, but agreed she had to do something. She gave her a list of local solicitors which she had acquired, and Mrs Kendrick chose one, and made an appointment. Once it was established that the situation was intolerable, an application was made at the local Magistrates Court for an ousting order pending a divorce application. Unfortunately Mrs Kendrick had to continue to live in the same house whilst the summons was served, and lived in fear of her husband's wrath.

CHAPTER 14

A week later Margaret sat with Mrs Kendrick until her husband came home from work. Mr Kendrick arrived home just after 6 o'clock. He was whistling as he came through the front door. He did not sound anything like the man his wife had described to the solicitor. Both the children had taken themselves upstairs.

'Hello,' he greeted Margaret. 'What do we owe this pleasure?' he continued. Margaret shifted in her chair before saying, 'Good evening Mr Kendrick. I wanted to talk to you.' She could almost feel Mrs Kendrick's nerves, and was sure she was shaking.

'Well fire away,' he said jovially. He oozed charm.

Margaret pointed to the envelope which had been placed on the dining table. 'Perhaps it would be best if you would read that summons.' The smile left his face and he followed her gaze to the dining table. A large brown envelope sat there. He went over and picked it up, he broke the seal and started to read. All his joviality disappeared as he read through the summons.

'Why this is preposterous,' he shouted. 'Whose idea was this?' he demanded.

'Mr Kendrick, perhaps I can explain,' she started. She stood up and suggested they all sit round the table to discuss it. Mrs Kendrick was very apprehensive, but went over and took one of the chairs. Mr Kendrick took the second chair, and Margaret followed.

'Your wife has found it extremely difficult to live with you for quite some time, and has decided that it is not possible to live with you anymore. She is frightened not only for herself but for the two children, who witness a lot of violence.' She explained. He sat motionless and said nothing.

'It had been suggested to her by her solicitor that she leave the house and take the children to a battered wives hostel, but I feel it would be better if they remained in the family home and you consider leaving voluntarily until the court hearing. How do you feel about that?' she said.

'It is a load of rubbish. I never hit her, she has had some bruises lately, but my wife is unsteady on her feet, and does not look where she is going, and hurts herself. Why only last week she fell over in the bathroom,' he shouted.

Mrs Kendrick, feeling braver and knowing she had to say something said, 'You know that is not true, you punched me and I fell against the wash basin. You were in one of your drunken rages and the children were watching. They can verify that.' She started to cry.

Margaret felt trapped between husband and wife, but soldiered on. 'Can we discuss this quietly, and try to find a way forward. If you feel unable to leave the house Mr Kendrick, your wife will have to request an ousting order which would be served on you, probably tomorrow, in the meantime I will take her and the children to a place of safety.'

He sat with his head in his hands for quite some while, then started to sob. A little while later he stood up and agreed to move out straightaway. Margaret said she would stay until he did. He went upstairs to collect some of his things, and returned with a packed holdall. As he went out of the front door he said he would be in touch.

Margaret felt relieved, and was pleased that she could now go home. She was already well over an hour late. She was not surprised that Gary was upset, and demanding to know why dinner was not ready. She took off her coat and assured him it would be ready soon. He was not impressed. 'Where have you been until now?' he demanded to know. She explained about her home visit and that she had needed to ensure that the husband left the house before she came home.

'It is not good enough, you are out all day, and you are forever having to see people in the evenings,' he ranted. It was no surprise to her that he then sulked for the rest of the evening, and did not say goodbye to her the following morning when going to start his taxi journeys. Life was getting worse. She wanted to do a good job, and she was sure she was, but Gary constantly reminded her she should be at home and not working. Well he would have to put up with it she decided, he was not prepared to understand.

The next morning a large brown envelope dropped on her doormat which was addressed to her and Gary. She opened it. It was an eviction notice from the building society.

She sat down and read the document carefully. They demanded vacation of the property (their house) within 28 days from the date of the order. She telephoned the building society, and pleaded with them to reconsider, but they were adamant. What was she to do. They would be homeless. She sat and thought for quite some while before getting the children up for school. She drove each to their respective schools, then took Katy to her mother's bungalow before driving onto the Council offices, situated in the town centre.

She went straight to the housing department and asked to see the housing officer. She was told she would have to make an appointment, but by chance the housing officer was just passing and had overheard she was desperate.

A lady came up to her and said to the clerk, 'It is all right Amanda I have a free half hour I will see this lady straightaway.' She smiled at Margaret and asked her to follow her down the corridor.

'How can I help?' she said. Margaret explained her dilemma. Miss Roache the housing officer listened without interrupting her, before asking her various questions. 'Where do you work?' she asked. Margaret told her she was employed by the County Council as a welfare officer, and that her husband's business was gradually folding because of the town redevelopment. That their livelihood was being eroded and out of their hands. The Sheriff of the County had demanded their town stand for demolition, the County Council were building a new town centre.

Miss Roache sat for a while before saying, 'I think I can help you Mrs Pearce. I am in charge of a few houses being kept for council workers, and school teachers. There is a four bedroom house available which you could move into fairly quickly, how does that sound?'

It was like music to her ears. Margaret could not believe it. The rent was quite reasonable and they would not have the mortgage payments to worry about. Although she wanted to own her own house, they were swamped with debt because of the taxi business. The taxis would have to go. Gary had not been in a good mood when he left for work, but with this on top he was going to be reprehensible.

Miss Roache smiled at her and started to fill in various forms. She told Margaret that they needed to be signed by Gary and herself and she would need the eviction notice to substantiate the application. Margaret accepted the forms and thanked the housing officer for seeing her so quickly and being so helpful.

She drove on to one of the big comprehensive schools, and started work for the day. At least they were not going to be homeless. What a day.

After checking the school registers she spent some time during the morning break talking to year heads about children with problems. She was told about a single parent who had five children who needed free meals and uniform grants, and that one of the children, a twelve year old boy had been seen by the Educational Psychologist and would have to be transferred to a special school for educationally subnormal children at Brighton. She drove to the terraced house just a few roads from the school. She knocked at the front door, which was opened by a woman in her late thirties. She explained why she had come, and was invited in.

Mrs Graham signed the forms for school meals and the uniform grants. Margaret explained that next term Billy her twelve year old would be going to St Cuthberts school at Brighton, and would stay there for half a term at a time.

'Oh that is a long way for him to go,' she remarked. You could see the concern in her face.

'Yes it is about fifty miles away, but I will be taking him in my car with two other children from this area,' Margaret explained. In essence none of the children liked going away from home, and often cried when they said goodbye to their families, but Margaret would put on a cassette and soon have them singing as they drove along, and once at the school they became involved in various activities. She assured Mrs Graham that Billy would be all right.

Her next visit was to a young girl who lived on the same council estate. She was an unmarried mum just 16 years of age. She had been having home tuition for a few hours a week, but now Pat Cook was old enough to work. She had two illegitimate sons Tim and Ben. Tim was just two years old and Pat could not cope with him. He shouted at her all the time, and she often smacked him, sometimes really hard. He used to scream, 'I hate you,' at her so the neighbours had stated. Pat had little money, and the house had bare floorboards. Margaret often took secondhand clothing round for the children, and sometimes for Pat herself.

Pat let her in, 'Maggie I don't think I can cope with Timmy any more, he is so awful.' After much discussion Margaret suggested that she refer Timmy to the Social Services department to decide what to do. She explained to Pat that perhaps she needed a break from the child, and that it might be best if he went into foster care.

'You'll have to do something, there are times I want to kill him,' she said. She then told Margaret she was once more pregnant again. Margaret despaired. She went home and typed out a referral to the children's department, suggesting at least for some respite care for Pat.

She then put the eviction notice on the table and prepared the dinner before going to collect the children from school and Katy. She did not tell her mother about the notice. She still did not think too highly of Gary, and did not want to rub salt into the wounds. Once back home, she was caught up in homework and washing as well as cooking the dinner.

Gary arrived home at half past five and she asked him to read the notice. He did not understand it and she had to spell it out to him. She then went on to tell him about her visit to the council offices and her interview with Miss Roache. He could not believe it, but was pleased that the house would be sold and all their debts paid up and they could start again in a council house. 'It's where we belong,' he told her. 'It was always good enough for my mother, and it is good enough for me.'

Margaret did not agree, but then went on to tell him that without their isolated house, and the redevelopment notice, the taxis would have to be sold, and he would have to find a job.

'You are joking,' he glared at her. 'I don't want a job. I have one.'

'Gary I am sorry to tell you this but it is true. I have been keeping the taxi business going for a long time now, subsidising what you earn to pay for the overheads, just ask the accountant.' She told him.

'I do not want to talk to him, he does not know what he is talking about,' he spat at her.

'Gary you have to listen to sense. I cannot support the business anymore. I work long hours and look after everyone in the family, and I cannot possibly do it anymore.'

He slammed out of the house and drove up the road at great speed. She knew it had been a hard pill to swallow, and he would need time to calm down. She gave the children their dinner, and by 8 o'clock they were all in bed. She wrote up her daily notes and went to bed herself by 9 o'clock, she was spent, absolutely exhausted. She left Gary's dinner in the oven on low heat. She heard him come in a little later, but pretended to be asleep when he came upstairs. She had nothing further to say to him.

CHAPTER 15

The following day, Gary was up early and had left the house before anyone else was up and about. Margaret was pleased, she knew Gary needed time to think through all what they had discussed the day before. She knew it would be hard for him.

She herself had a very busy day ahead. The Kendricks' preliminary court case was to be heard at the local county court that morning and she had promised to attend. After getting all the children ready for school, and Katy ready to go to playschool, she checked through her paperwork to ensure she had everything she needed in her briefcase.

It was a bright sunny morning, and her heart felt light. They had somewhere to live, and after the court hearing she was collecting the key to the house on the council estate, from the council offices. She had to pay two weeks rent in advance, but this was nothing in comparison to the monthly mortgage payments. They had three more weeks at their house, and hopefully Gary would help her box things up and start to sell the taxis and equipment. It would be sad to say goodbye to some of the drivers, who she had become friendly with over the last few years, but it could not be helped.

Mr Kendrick was already at the court, when she arrived with his wife, who was feeling extremely nervous and was glad of some support. The matter was heard in chambers, and after hearing the facts the Judge made an order that Mr Kendrick would not visit the house, nor be within 500 yards of it. He then set the divorce hearing aside to be heard in two months time. Mr Kendrick had agreed to the order, and gave his address as a local hostel for men. She learnt that his employer, having heard about the case and the fact that he was drinking excessively had given him notice, and he was now looking for another job. She hoped he would consider taking up her suggestion to join Alcoholics Anonymous to help him conquer his drinking problem. She knew he would also get some counselling which would be helpful. He needed a job quite quickly so that he could pay maintenance for the children, but in the meantime she would help Mrs Kendrick apply for DHSS benefits.

She left the court house and drove to the council offices, and after paying two weeks rent in advance she accepted the keys to number 7 Stanton Road, a four bedroomed house on four levels. On arriving at the house she opened the front door and looked around. It was a very unusual house. On the ground floor, on the outside was a large garage, and inside was a downstairs cloakroom. On mounting six stairs she entered the kitchen diner, a very large room with the kitchen at one end. An outside door led to the small garden.

She returned to the stairwell, and climbed eight more stairs, where she opened the door leading into the large lounge. A very spacious room with big windows letting in lots of light. A further eight stairs led up to the bathroom and the first bedroom. It was quite spacious and would suit one of the children, possibly Anne. Eight more stairs led to the largest bedroom which had lots of fitted wardrobes and like the lounge had large windows. This would obviously be her and Gary's bedroom.

Eight more stairs led to two more bedrooms. The first was very small with only room for a single bed and chest of drawers, but the other was big enough for twin beds as well as furniture. This room would be suitable for Sarah and Katy, and Peter could have the small bedroom. Goodness what a large house. She descended the stairs and checked out cupboards and plugs in the kitchen before leaving. Yes Gary would approve she was sure. She made her way to a local junior school who had requested she visit urgently.

On arrival she was shown into the headteacher's office. 'Ah Mrs Pearce, I am so glad you have come so quickly.' He said. Mr Knight was a very pleasant man who was adored by all the children in his school. He was extremely kind and Margaret had noticed on previous visits how the children often followed him around.

'We have a problem on our hands, a little girl called Penny Long. Her mother is a single parent, who is known to have 'boyfriends', but Penny's teacher has been concerned for some time because Penny comes to school inadequately clothed for the cold weather, and the thin plimsolls she wears have holes in them.' He told her.

'I see, well I can call and see her mother and see what can be done to help the situation Mr Knight,' she suggested.

'Good,' he started. 'But that is not all, I called in the Medical Officer this morning because Penny has a nasty burn mark on her right shoulder, and will not say how it got there.'

'Well under the Child Protection rules I must report this to Social Services, and make an urgent visit to see Mrs Long. Firstly, I would like to see Penny before I go to see her mother, if this can be arranged?'

'Certainly, I will fetch Penny myself. She is a nervous little thing, and it would be best if I stay with her if you do not mind Mrs Pearce?'

'I would be most grateful if you would Mr Knight, you obviously know the child well?'

He left his office, and very shortly returned with a little girl of about eight years of age. She was so thin and rather grubby. She had on a summer dress and no cardigan. Margaret felt cold for her.

She smiled at the child and let Mr Knight take the lead. He told Penny that Mrs Pearce was calling to see her mother and try and arrange for some nice warm clothing to be acquired. Penny put her thumb in her mouth, saying nothing.

Margaret asked her what she liked about school, and gradually the child started to give small answers. 'I like the dinners,' she said. 'I like painting,' and 'I like the stories the teacher tells us.'

Now she had the child talking Margaret ventured to ask if she could see the mark on her shoulder which the doctor had looked on earlier. The child was immediately on guard, but with a little bit of coaxing she opened the top of her dress, where a long narrow burn mark was clearly evident. 'How did this happen Penny?' she asked.

The child's eyes opened wide with fear. Her thumb returned to her mouth. She would say no more. Mr Knight took her back to her class, and returned to his office once more.

'She is a poorly little thing, she often smells of urine and is very often very hungry, she has been caught raiding the school tuck shop some mornings. The staff are very good to her and will wash her down and make sure she has a good dinner each day; but something is terribly wrong,' he explained.

'Fine, well I will go straightaway and see her mother,' Margaret told him, and departed. She drove to a local council estate which was known locally as the single parent estate, as most houses were given over to one parent families.

She knocked on the door of number 20 Bowen Close. The door was opened by a young woman about 30 years of age. 'Hello Mrs Long,' Margaret said, 'I am the local Education Welfare Officer, and I would like to talk to you about Penny.' The woman seemed a bit reluctant but invited her in. it was a very cold day outside, but in the lounge a small fire was burning. The furniture was sparse, just a small table and chairs, and a large sofa was all that were in the room.

Mrs Long did not suggest she sat down, so Margaret moved some items on the sofa and sat down. 'I am aware you are a single parent, and that money is scarce, but it has been noticed at school that Penny has very inadequate clothing.' She saw the woman relax. 'Yes I cannot afford to buy her any warm clothing, what she has on I got from a jumble sale, for a few pennies,' she told Margaret.

'I see, well perhaps I can help here. I have some funds which can be used to buy a few essential items. Unfortunately she will not qualify for a uniform grant until she becomes eleven. We get clothing handed in at various schools and I am sure I can find a coat and a couple of warm cardigans, and the school fund will let me have some money for a pair of shoes for her.'

'Oh that would be great, thank you very much,' the woman rose. Margaret sat where she was. 'Mrs Long, I am also concerned about the burn mark on Penny's shoulder. Can you tell me how it got there?'

The woman froze. She started twisting her hands. She then started to cry. Margaret opened her bag and produced a tissue.

A little later the woman took Margaret upstairs and showed her a single sized mattress on a bed. It was soaking wet. There were no sheets or blankets on the bed. 'Penny wets the bed and just look at the state of the mattress. If I smack her it makes no difference, she does it all the more. My boyfriends spank her and send her upstairs without any tea, but she still does it. I lost my temper yesterday, and hit her with the poker. I regretted it as soon as I had done it, and swore her to secrecy. I gave her some sweets, but I could do nothing about the burn mark. I bathed it but it made her scream, in the end I put on some soothing cream.'

'I see, well Mrs Long I am afraid I will have to report the matter to the Social Services Department, and a case conference will be convened to discuss the matter. I will be in touch shortly.' Margaret left the house and went to collect Katy from the playschool before driving home. She typed out her report, sent a copy to head office, and a copy to the Social Services. She telephoned that department and requested a case conference. There was no more she could do. What a busy day it had been.

She went to the local supermarket and acquired some large cardboard boxes which she flattened, before collecting the children from their schools; returning home and cooking the dinner.

Gary arrived just after six o'clock, in a reasonably cheerful mood. She told him she had been to see the house, and he agreed to go with her the following day to look round. He removed the flattened boxes from the boot of her car and got them ready to fill with household items. That night he made love to her, she had to admit that he tried hard to show he cared about her, he held her in his arms and kissed her deeply, whispering how lucky they were, but even with his best efforts, she felt very unloved. She laid awake thinking about this while he laid sprawled across her, completely sated, and gently snoring. Sleep evaded her.

The following day she was notified by the Social Services Department that there was to be a case conference that afternoon at 3pm to discuss Penny Long. Her whole day would have to be altered. She sped through her morning schedule visiting the local schools and checking the registers, dashed home at lunchtime for a sandwich and prepared the evening meal. At 3pm she arrived at the Social

Services Department along with representatives from the police, Penny's school and the health visitor for the area. The medical officer and a probation officer also attended.

As she had made the referral Margaret explained her visit to the school, and her contact with Penny and later the child's mother. Mr Knight explained how he had followed procedure and had notified her as well as requesting that the medical officer look at the injury. The probation officer said he knew Mrs Long quite well mainly due to the fact that her men friends were often known to the probation department, and had form. The health visitor said she had not seen Penny for two years, but was always concerned about the care her mother gave her, and that her mother being a single parent often had different boyfriends at the house.

It was agreed that the child was at risk of further injury, and that a place of safety order would be applied for. A social worker would be taking on the case. The chairman thanked Margaret for her referral, and advised her she would be required to attend court to give evidence shortly. Miss Briggs the social worker would apply for a court order that day and the child would be placed in a children's home.

Margaret worried about Penny, she was such a nervous little thing and asked if she could take the child to the children's home. it was agreed that she could but the social worker must go as well.

Margaret felt exasperated after all she was a welfare officer, why could she not take the child, but rules were rules, as the Chairman told her she would have to be a qualified social worker if she wanted to see cases right through.

She dashed home and put the dinner on, checked the children were doing their homework, and when Gary came in she told him she had to go out again. He was furious. 'Where are you off to now?' he shouted at her.

'I have to go with a small child to the other side of Winchester, she will be scared going with someone strange.' She replied, and not bothering to turn around grabbed her coat and flew out of the front door. There had been no time for her to have any dinner, she was picking up the social worker at 6.30pm and going straight round to Bowen Close to collect Penny.

The social worker showed Ms Long the court order, and Margaret helped Jenny put some of the clothes into a carrier bag, before they departed and drove to Romsey. They stopped off on the journey at a fish and chip shop, and ate in the car. They were all hungry.

The social worker advised Margaret that the court hearing requesting a Care Order be made in respect of the child would be in a few weeks time, and she would confirm the date and time.

******

She was enjoying the lectures at the college and any spare moment she had was geared to learning. She absorbed all she was taught, and read countless books to do with Government and Children's welfare. She had lots of essays to do which she often completed late at night. Although Gary was preoccupied with coming to terms with giving up the taxis and finding a job, she had to admit he put a lot of effort into packing things ready for the move, which she was grateful for.

One of the taxi firm rivals came forward and agreed to buy the hackney plates and the wedding cars were soon sold almost within a week. Now she would have to arrange for new schools for the children. Stanton Road was on the other side of town. Sarah being so good at her academic studies, Margaret was not happy that she attend the nearest Comprehensive school to Stanton Road, it did not have a very good reputation, but as it was the catchment school so there seemed little choice.

Christmas was not far away, but she had far too much to think about at present, to give it any thought. She liked to make the Christmas cake and Christmas puddings, and prepare some small presents for the children. Once the move was complete, she would organise things.

The move went really well. The children were pleased with the house, there was lots of room, and although Sarah had to share with Katy, they each had their own space. Anne loved her own room, she had always shared with Sarah and Peter had always shared with Katy. There was room for Margaret to have a desk in the lounge. However she was not happy with the neighbourhood. There were many large families living in the vicinity. Milk was often stolen from their doorstep, and children played out in the street, teenage boys had motorcycles racing up and down the road, you could not call it peaceful.

It was not long before she decided that although the house was comfortable, she would want to move away from the area as soon as possible. She kept these thoughts to herself as she knew Gary would not agree with her. He was used to living on a council estate before she married him. He was in his element living at Stanton Road.

Why was life such a challenge? she thought. *Why did she feel she had to fight her way through life? Why couldn't life be so much easier?*

CHAPTER 16

Within a week of moving, Gary had found himself a job at a local manufacturers of farm equipment. It was not well paid but it was a regular job. He told her that it was a fairly easy job in the storeroom. He would work just a five day week from 8am - 6pm. Well at least he had a job, and although he said he missed the taxi business and being his own boss, he felt under less pressure. The owner of the taxi firm which bought the hackney plates offered Gary a few hours part time driving which he jumped at.

Margaret spent hours sewing and putting up curtains, fitting carpet, and arranging their furniture in all the rooms. With Gary being at home at weekends she was able to leave quite a few things with him to do. There had been no need to decorate, all the walls were painted with magnolia emulsion, but they had bought lots of stair carpet for the many short flights of stairs.

Margaret had already given up hiring wedding dresses, and gradually she advertised them and they were sold for a small amount of money. Peter and Sarah seemed happy at their new school. Anne had remained at her old school as she was due to leave school the following Easter, and there seemed no point in moving her.

Before she could turn round Christmas was upon them, and she was busy preparing for the event. Now free of all the financial burdens she was able to indulge the children with nice presents that year. Anne wanted some up to date clothes, which she chose herself, Peter wanted a bicycle, but Sarah preferred to have some money, some to spend and some to save. Katy wanted a new doll with pretty clothes.

The festive season was quite fun and Margaret enjoyed cooking the Christmas Dinner before sitting down to watch the Queen's Speech on the television and put her feet up. Gary had bought her a pair of gloves, which she badly needed, and she bought him a shirt and tie. Everyone seemed happy. *Perhaps things were getting better at last,* she thought.

The journey to Southampton was rather treacherous during the months of January and February with snow and ice on the roads, there were some days she dreaded going, but she persevered. The class was advised that they would be required to spend a residential weekend at a hotel in the New Forest during the month of April. This would mean arriving on a Friday morning and leaving on a Sunday afternoon. The object was for the class to spend more time together, as well as working until 6pm each day on certain projects. Gary was not impressed when she told him, but as she pointed out to him he was home at weekends mostly and it would not really be a problem. He finally acquiesced.

In April Anne left school and found a job at the local veterinary surgery. It was lowly pay, but to her it was a fortune. As she did not work at weekends either she told Margaret she would help look after the other children for a couple of days, while she was away. Anne loved animals and had always wanted to work with them. Part of her job was to hold the animals while they were being treated by the vet. Unfortunately this often meant she was scratched badly by cats and bitten by dogs. So Margaret often had to take her to hospital to have either an injection of penicillin or a tetanus jab.

One day Anne came home accompanied by a large ginger coloured mongrel on a lead. 'Who's dog is that?' Margaret asked. Anne looked a little sheepish, then said she had been asked to put the dog down, but could not do it. She had decided that she could find a home for the dog locally. She pleaded with her mother to let the dog stay the night and she would find it a good home. Margaret agreed, and that evening Anne went out trying hard to find a home for the dog. Unfortunately she arrived home at 10pm and admitted defeat. She pleaded with her mother to let the dog stay another day, but Margaret was adamant. She had to return the dog to the surgery. Anne was in tears, but Margaret stood firm. They already had a dog, and two was too many. Reluctantly Anne agreed to take the dog back the following day.

The following week Margaret packed a small suitcase with a few clothes and put her briefcase and notepad into the car ready for her residential course. She was quite excited, although apprehensive at leaving the children. Having left full instructions on what was for meals and how to contact her if there was a problem, she set off. It was a lovely sunny day and she felt content as she drove down the M3 motorway towards the New Forest. She had been given directions of where the hotel was, and she soon found it just before Lyndhurst. There were lots of ponies wandering across the land on either side of the road. It was beautiful, just like a picture postcard. She pulled into the car park, and immediately was hailed by Andrea. 'Hi, I hope if we have to share a room we will be together,' she said to Margaret. They walked up the steps into the foyer where a lot of their classmates were standing around chatting. Everyone greeted them. They were then given a room number. Unfortunately Andrea was placed with Thora who she knew quite well, and Margaret was to share with Jenny and Dawn. Their room was in an annex, but was a very large room and had two single beds and a small cot bed. They decided to draw straws who would sleep in the cot bed, which turned out that Jenny drew the short straw. She looked most unhappy. It was laughable because Jenny was very tall and fairly stocky, so in the end Margaret offered to swap with her, being quite small it seemed appropriate.

Coffee was served and they moved into the conference room for their first lecture. At lunch time they sat in the dining room and were served a very nice salad, before once more returning to the conference room. Everyone felt sleepy, but it turned out to be a very interesting discussion on fostering and adoption which Margaret found fascinating. She could equate with the subject, having been fostered herself during the war when she had been evacuated to North Wales, at such a young age.

The three course evening meal was very nice, and one of the group Ben splashed out on a couple of bottles of wine for them. Everyone was in good spirits.

It was agreed that when the meal was finished they would all go for a walk, which they did, returning to the hotel about 10pm. They were all merry having popped in to the local pub for a drink in the village. Jenny and Ben had played darts, and on the way back they had been singing one or two popular songs. As they approached the hotel they could see that the outdoor swimming pool was all lit up.

Ben said, 'What say you all we go for a swim?' Most people were up for it. One lady on the course who was usually very prim suddenly ran toward the pool and started stripping off her outer clothes. She climbed up to the diving board in just her bra and corset, what a sight she was. Everyone started laughing and egging her on. She dived into the water to much applause. One or two others joined her including Ben, who was always up for any fun. Margaret and Andrea watched. No one had any towels, and when they finally all climbed out of the pool they realised only too well they had to go into the hotel as they were dripping wet.

The following day the tutors suggested that if anyone wanted to use the pool to ensure they had towels with them. Saturday followed the same pattern as the day before, but no one ventured into the pool that night, though most people went into the village after dinner. Margaret learnt how to play darts.

On the Sunday afternoon after the plenary session she drove home, to be greeted by very inquisitive children. She explained about all the lectures but omitted to tell them of the exploits which went on. Gary seemed to have missed her and was glad she was back. He was very attentive, he had listened to all she had told them about the weekend without passing comment. They all sat down to Sunday tea, Katy snuggling up to her mother. Katy had missed her probably the most. It was a nice feeling that they all needed her.

It was later that evening when the children had all gone to bed when he asked, 'You won't be going away again will you?'

'Probably not,' she replied. 'But I did enjoy it Gary and I learnt a lot. We have exams coming up in just a few weeks time, and I do want to do well.'

The following day while she was working she received a telephone call from Tom her colleague. 'Maggie I have been down to Cornwall for a couple of weeks with Jenny and we have decided to get married in June.'

'Congratulations Tom, I look forward to meeting Jenny, is she coming to live up here?' she asked.

'I am afraid not, I have applied for a transfer to Bodmin, there is a post available down there. Jenny has her dance studio and would prefer to live there, so it looks like I will be moving there in the very near future,' he replied.

'Oh Tom, I will miss you, what rotten luck for me.' Though she knew Gary would be pleased, he did not like Tom. That meant there would be a new colleague joining her in Harmsworth.

She drove to the school Anne had recently left. The headmaster had telephoned her to say he was excluding a boy for bad behaviour, and for swearing at the headteacher. He had listed him to receive the cane as punishment, but the boy had refused, so the headmaster had no alternative but to report the matter to the school governors and suspend him. After some discussion Margaret agreed to visit the boy at home and talk with his parents.

Later that day she called at his home. His father was at work, but his mother Mrs Baxter told Margaret his father backed the boy, no caning, they would take him to a different school. Margaret talked to the boy Brian and pointed out that another school may not accept him. She then went on to talk with him about the incident. Brian admitted that on reflection he had been wrong, and was sorry about swearing at the headmaster.

'Do you miss your friends at school Brian?' she asked him.

'Yes I do, and some of the local lads poke fun at me because I have been excluded,' he told her.

'Don't you think it would be better to apologise to the headteacher, and take your punishment, then you can go back to school? I will come with you,' she coaxed.

He sat and thought for a while, and then agreed. She telephoned the school and made an appointment for Brian to see the headteacher the following day.

Another success she thought. The following week she saw him in the school corridor, when he smiled at her, she smiled back, nothing more was said. It was over.

The examinations loomed large. Three exams, what a challenge. *I can only do my best* she thought, hoping with all her might she would pass. She remembered that if she failed one she failed them all, and would have to retake them the following year, along with the other three subjects they would be studying as from September.

She studied most evenings after the children were in bed and any spare hours at the weekends. She was determined to do her best.

CHAPTER 17

It was a beautiful June morning, there were no clouds in the sky and the sun was just rising as Margaret drove along the M3 motorway toward Southampton. It was the first day of the examinations. Her mind was in a whirl, the exam today was Central Government and would be three hours long. She quizzed herself on historical dates as she drove along. The examinations were to be held in the huge hall of the Southampton Institute next to the College of Technology.

She felt very nervous on entering the building, and even more so when shown into the examination room. All the desks were set out separately in rows, and each one had on it a sheet of paper with the questions on it. Having left her handbag on a table near the door, she made her way to the desk with her number on it, and sat down.

Other members of her course gradually filtered in, and people smiled at each other. No talking was allowed. At precisely 9am the Adjudicator told them they could turn over their paper and start, and that the bell would go at precisely 12 noon. Margaret turned over the paper and started reading.

Some three hours later the bell went. She had answered all the questions and hoped she had given the right answers. Everyone headed for the refectory and a well earned lunch. Margaret sat with Jenny and Dawn, the entire conversation being how everyone had perceived the questions. She returned to Harmsworth during the afternoon feeling absolutely shattered. Monday was never her best day of the week. But she knew the next two days she had to repeat the process as there were two more exams to take. She decided to go straight home and complete some overdue paperwork for head office before collecting the children. As she drove to her mothers to collect Katy she was miles away in her mind when a police officer on a motorcycle overtook her and requested her to pull over. She pulled over to the kerb.

He got off his motorcycle and came up to her driver's door, she wound down the window. 'Do you realise you were exceeding the speed limit Madam?' he asked her. She was totally unaware she had been speeding.

'I am sorry officer, I had not realised I was in the 30 mile an hour zone.' She told him. He lectured her on keeping within the limit, and said on this occasion he would just warn her. She thanked him and promised to be more careful in future. He put on his helmet and got back on his motorcycle.

She realised her mind was thinking about the exams she would have to be more careful. She did not tell Gary about that incident, and he seemed distracted and uninterested in her day.

Tuesday and Wednesday followed a very similar pattern, and by Wednesday afternoon she was exhausted. She still had two full days work to complete a whole week's work.

At least college was finished until September and all she had to do now was wait for the results of the examinations, which should come through by August.

When Gary arrived home that night she suggested that they take a week's holiday, and suggested they hire a caravan and tow it down to Dawlish in Devon and pitch up at a caravan park. It would not cost too much money. The only expense was having a tow bar attached to the back of her Vauxhall Cresta car.

They booked a caravan for the last week in July. Anne decided she would prefer to stay with her friend Tess. They had been friends for years, both attending the same school. Tess often came to their house and sometimes stayed for a meal. Margaret liked the girl and knew Anne would be fine with Tess's family.

The children looked forward to this break and helped Margaret pack their clothes. There was all the food to be prepared, the caravan would have a fridge and a larder. They certainly would not want to buy meals out which could be expensive for all of them. Margaret did not feel confident about driving towing the caravan, so Gary drove all the way. Unfortunately, they were late arriving at the caravan site, and all the best places were taken. The man at the gate told Gary he would have to park up in the back field. When they drove into the field they realised it was on a slope. Another man explained they would have to park sideways and prop one of the wheels up with bricks to stop it rolling down the hill. Margaret was aghast.

However, the man showed them how he had propped his own caravan up and it seemed okay so they went along with it. For two days all was well, but on the third day everything started to go wrong. Early in the morning, Sarah went off to the wash room and shortly afterwards someone ran and told Margaret that Sarah had fainted and was laying on the concrete floor. Margaret dashed to the wash room. Sarah was just coming round, but it was obvious that she had a raging temperature. Sarah was prone to tonsillitis, as well as colds and flu. Margaret helped her back to the caravan, gave her a junior disprin and put her to bed.

It started to rain and the ground around the caravan started to get very muddy and slippery. Gary had gone to find Peter. Sarah was feeling a little brighter and was playing outside the caravan with Katy under the awning. Suddenly the caravan started to lurch sideways, and the next minute Margaret stared in horror as the caravan started to roll slowly down the hill. She ran and moved the children out of the way.

The bricks had moved in the soft ground. Two men ran over and stopped the caravan in its track. Gary arrived with Peter and the three men together managed to turn the van. Gary started the car and pulled round in front of the caravan and hitched it up.

They moved it down to the bottom of the slope and wedged it against the hedge. Once more it was bricked up but on firmer ground. Margaret was afraid to sleep in the van that night, fearful it would roll again, but it stayed firm. On the other hand Sarah's fever started up again and Margaret knew she needed to see a doctor. The following morning she learnt the nearest doctor was in a village some five miles from the camp site.

She returned to the caravan and told Gary to pack up everything they were going home.

'But we have paid for a whole week's rent of the pitch,' he yelled at her.

'It can't be helped, Sarah is ill, I want to take her home,' she replied.

'Peter wanted to go back down to the beach. Katy wanted to play. What a nightmare.

'I can't sleep in the caravan I keep thinking it will roll, and it is too damp for Sarah with such a high temperature,' she finally flung at Gary. 'I want to go home.'

She was near to tears and eventually Gary agreed to decamp and within an hour they had started on their way home. What a terrible holiday it had been.

They arrived home late that Wednesday evening, and gradually Margaret put Sarah to bed before unpacking the caravan. The following day Gary took the caravan back to the hire garage and Margaret called the doctor out. He soon determined that Sarah had tonsillitis and prescribed some penicillin. Within two days she was much better. As Gary was on leave from work for the week, he made himself useful around the house and washing her car which was caked with mud.

Lots of mail had arrived whilst they were away, and Margaret opened it gradually. It was mostly bills and advertisements, but one brown envelope stood out. It was addressed to her personally. She opened it to find it was her exam results. She had passed on Central Government and Local Government but failed on Child Welfare. *Oh no, she thought, if I fail one I fail them all, she remembered what the tutor had said.* She sat down with a heavy heart. All that work, all that studying, how could she have failed her best subject Child Welfare? *I am a failure* she started to cry.

Gary found her crying, and wanted to know what was wrong. She showed him the result form. 'I have failed,' she told him.

'Well it is not the end of the world, you still have a job, now perhaps you will agree it is too much for you and concentrate on your family instead of all this studying,' he was smiling as he said this. She felt so angry. Angry with herself, and angry with him, for not understanding. It had felt like the worst week of her life.

She was glad when the week ended and she went back to work. She rang Andrea and told her the bad news, who promptly said, 'Look, the tutor said you can retake these three examinations next year as well as the other three subjects. You can do it, Oh Maggie please think about it. I know it will be hard but we will all help you, if we can.'

Margaret thanked her for her kindness and felt a little cheered. She would think about it.

Sarah went to stay with her mother for a few weeks, and Katy went most weekdays. Peter kept himself busy. He did a paper round each morning, and often cleaned his bike, or had it in pieces, oiling it. He often mended his friends' bikes too, he was quite good at it.

Gary went back to work the following week and she went back to doing home visits now that the schools were closed for the holidays. There were lots of uniform grants to deliver, and employment cards to write out under the Employment of Children act.

She had received a message from the area officer that a nine year old boy had been killed on the railway line. He and some friends had apparently been playing chicken when an express train had hit him and killed him. He had been attending the local junior school along with his brother and sister and they were all on free school meals, as his parents Mr and Mrs Coombs were poor. She remembered the family who lived in Beale Way. Derek was the middle child and had been extremely lively.

The message advised her that now there was only two children in the family they did not qualify for free school meals. She had to go and tell them. *Oh Lord* she thought, and immediately decided to leave the matter for the time being. She would call in a couple of weeks time.

One afternoon the doorbell rang, and she found on her doorstep the big tall policeman who had stopped her along Perrin Road a few weeks before.

'Ah Mrs Pearce, I am told you authorise work permits for children, is that so?' he enquired.

'Yes that is part of my job,' she replied.

'Well I wonder if you could help me. My son Andrew has been doing a paper round for nearly a year now and was stopped this morning by a colleague of mine, who found he had no work permit. Is it possible I could ask you to kindly let him have one?' he asked. She suddenly thought the situation funny. Here was this big police officer pleading with her to make his son legal.

She went to her desk and picked up a form and gave it to him. 'Please have your son complete the form and arrange to give it to me when I visit his school when it opens in a few weeks. In the meantime, as he is over fourteen, and providing he does not work more than two hours a day, he can continue until I give him a permit. I will be in touch with the newsagent; he should not have employed him without a permit.'

'Thank you so much Mrs Pearce, you are most kind. He is a good lad and did not realise what he should do.' He moved towards the door. She opened the door for him and smiled Whew, she had thought he had come about her speeding. She wondered if he remembered her. Well one good turn deserved another.

Two weeks were soon up and time was moving on, she plucked up courage to visit Mary Coombs about the death of Derek. She drove to the house in Beale Way, and walked up the front path, not knowing what to say to the woman.

The woman opened the door in response to her knock and invited her in. Margaret was about to speak when Mary Coombs suddenly said, 'Thank you for coming to see me, no one comes near. Everyone seems scared to visit me, I have never felt so lonely.'

Margaret said how sorry she was to have learnt about Derek, and then again felt lost for words. Mary said, 'Mrs Pearce would you be kind enough to come upstairs with me and help me put Derek's things away I can't do it.' Margaret was taken aback, but agreed to go with the woman. It took nearly an hour to bag up his clothes and toys, stripping the bed and dismantling the bed. His brother could now have a much larger room.

They went downstairs, and Mary put the kettle on. It was then that Margaret plucked up the courage to tell Mary the reason for her visit.

'Mary I am afraid that because of the accident to Derek, you do not qualify for free school meals with just two children; I am so sorry.' She sat nervously on a kitchen chair.

'Mrs Pearce I am so glad you came. Everyone is avoiding me, they do not know what to say to me. The least of my worries is that we will have to pay for school dinners. But thank you so much for your help today, we will find the money for the meals.' She handed Margaret a mug of tea, and they both sat for some while thinking. *How strange*, she thought, *I was so worried about coming, and now I am glad I did.*

Margaret drove home feeling perplexed. She encountered so many situations for which she had no real training to cope, but she managed. She may not have passed her exams but she felt she was a good welfare officer. Yes Andrea was right, she must strive to pass all her exams next year, it was another challenge.

CHAPTER 18

The new school term started at the beginning of September. There was much to do. She would be returning to college in two weeks time, and in the meantime there were lots of schools to visit and home visits to parents.

Margaret had been visiting a lady who had been referred to her from the battered wives' hostel. Joan Beak was in her forties and married with three children, Terry, Linda and Roy. Joan had been at the hostel with her children for some weeks, scared to return home because her husband had been violent, and she was afraid for her life and the lives of her children. Margaret was sure he would not have harmed the children, but she was cautious, knowing the circumstances.

Ed Beak was a very big man, well o ver six feet tall, and very broad. He argued with his wife constantly over really petty things. Most arguments ended up with him striking her. She was a nervous wreck. Nothing pleased the man. The children got on his nerves, he often smashed anything in his hand such as plates and mugs, and he had been known to throw a knife. It would appear that his employer had found him to be rather lazy and given him the sack. He could not get another job without a decent reference. He blamed Joan for his having been late for work some mornings, when really he had overslept, often staying up most of the night watching films on the television.

The second day of the new term, Margaret was called to one of the comprehensive schools. Terry had told his teacher that his father had waylaid them on their way back to the hostel from school the day before, and demanded to know where their mother was. Terry was scared his father would follow them to the hostel. She told them she would collect them that afternoon, and take them back to the hostel and arrange to see their father. Later that day she called at the family home to see Ed, but he was not at home.

The following day she received a telephone call from the local police station. Ed had locked himself in the family house with his German Shepherd dog. The police had surrounded the house, Ed was upstairs at one of the bedroom windows, threatening all sorts of things apparently. He had demanded to see Margaret. He would only speak to her so he said.

So she drove to the Willard estate where the house was situated. A policeman met her as she got out of her car and recounted what had been going on. She walked up the garden path with him, and the back door opened a slit. Ed stood there with the huge dog. 'Only Mrs Pearce can come in,' he said. The policeman backed off, and left her there. She felt quite nervous, but all she could do was go in.

She kept a wary eye on the dog. She did not like Alsatians, and they seemed to know it. She moved into the lounge and sat down on the settee.

'Now Mr Beak, or can I call you Ed?' she asked him. The big man sat down. He put his head in his hands, 'What have I done?' he said. 'My wife does not want me, my children are afraid of me, and my boss has given me the sack.' He continued, 'we were getting in debt, and Joan spurns me. I just want to end it all.' Tears flowed down his cheeks. His dog sensed something was wrong with his master and glared at her. She sat and talked with Ed for nearly an hour, whilst the police still remained outside.

He finally agreed to Margaret arranging for him to see Joan so that they could talk. She knew there was a room at the Court House which was used by the Probation Dept for mitigation meetings, which she could use, on the proviso he left the children alone. She also pointed out to him that the council house was provided for the family and that Joan and the children should return there when it was safe to do so. He would have to find somewhere to live. He told her he had slept rough a few nights but now had some lodgings in the town. She noted the address and told him she would be in contact with him soon.

He finally agreed to leave the house. He was holding her hand when he went out through the back door and told the police he would keep away in future. He just wanted to see his children regularly and talk with his wife, and that Mrs Pearce was arranging this. Margaret assured them she would be working with the family and hopefully there would be an amicable outcome. The police secured the back door, and told Ed they would give him a lift to his lodgings.

Margaret went to see Joan and told her what had been happening, and she eventually agreed to a meeting with Ed. She had contacted the Probation Offices and booked a meeting room for the following week, which she would attend with Ed and Joan. Joan had already started divorce proceedings with the help of the residential social worker at the hostel, and requested custody of the children. It was just a matter of Ed coming to terms with the events. As far as Joan was concerned, she wanted nothing more to do with him, but agreed he could see the children from time to time.

Margaret was working extremely hard as Tom had moved down to Cornwall during the summer holiday, and there was no replacement for him at present, although the post was advertised. So her days became longer, much to Gary's annoyance.

One evening that week she attended Sarah's new school with Gary for Parents Evening. She knew Sarah was very bright, and hoped she had settled in well.

The year head shook hands with them and started shuffling paper about. 'Ah yes Sarah,' he started. 'She is a very pleasant pupil but not doing very well.' He continued.

Margaret asked him questions about certain subjects, which he appeared not to be able to answer. Margaret was getting cross. He was uncomfortable answering her questions.

'Mr Jackson can you describe our daughter?' she asked. Mr Jackson looked confused before saying, 'I am afraid not, I just have these comments by various teachers about her, I think she is doing reasonably well. I will look into it.'

Margaret stood up. 'Either you are wasting my time or I am wasting yours,' she could hear her voice rising. 'I know my daughter is doing well, we needed to know how she had settled in, but you do not know or even know who she is,' she shouted. She stormed out of the hall, with Gary following her.

'I am arranging to have Sarah moved to another school,' she told Gary as they made their way back home.

'But why?' he asked.

'Because I want the best for our daughter, she is a very clever girl, her last school told me so. She is never going to do well here, is she?' she asked him.

'I suppose not. You know best,' he replied.

So the following day she contacted the Education Officer and requested a transfer for Sarah to what was then the Grammar School. The school was approached, having read her school reports, and within two weeks Sarah moved to The John Wesley school.

Having started back at college she was once more studying, this time it was Sociology, English, Psychology and the workings of the Social Services Department. She also had to revise the three previous subjects, ready to take all six exams the following year. *I must be mad* she thought.

A communiqué from Head Office told her they had appointed two more Education Welfare Officers. The town of Harmsworth was growing so fast with the many London overspill families, that the department had decided the boundaries should be changed, so her area decreased in size. This was good news. So there were to be three welfare officers for the area.

During that week she met both Jim Forbes and Zoe Fox. She had been asked to show them round and make them feel welcome. She introduced them to the headteachers of the schools in their area and to other community workers who she knew. It was also decided that a new area manager would be appointed, but it had to be someone who was qualified. Unfortunately she still had not passed her exams. So within a month a very elderly man who she knew from the County Meetings was coming to be in charge at Harmsworth. He was near retirement age, but a very knowledgeable man.

She was called to give evidence at the County Court house in respect of the Kendrick family. Mrs Kendrick had applied for a divorce and custody of her children, and it was being contested by Mr Kendrick.

His solicitor asked her why Mr Kendrick could not be considered for joint custody of his children. Margaret explained to the Judge of her involvement, and the worries Mrs Kendrick had for the children, not only for their physical wellbeing but also for their mental wellbeing. The judge listened patiently, and after retiring for a short while came back and made an order for a decree nisi and granting custody to Mrs Kendrick, with reasonable access to their father, which may need to be supervised.

Mrs Kendrick was overjoyed, and hugged Margaret outside the Court House. 'Thank you so much for your support Maggie, I could not have done it without you,' she said. 'I have made a will that if anything happens tome the children will go to live with my sister in South Africa. The children are going to spend a couple of weeks with her at Christmas. I have a little job now and I can afford the fare for them,' she told Margaret.

'Wow that sounds great, are you sure you shouldn't be going with them?' she asked.

Mrs Kendrick replied, 'No they will be fine and I will continue to work. My sister will meet them at the airport and they will be fine with her.'

But Margaret felt unconvinced, the woman was pale and careworn she could do with some nice warm sunny weather. It would be hot and sunny in December in South Africa and a rest would do her a lot of good. But she could not persuade Mrs Kendrick to go. The college work was going well, and in early October her tutor told the class that they would be going for a few days residential stay at a local convent, about five miles from the college. *Oh Lord,* she thought. *Gary was not going to be pleased at my going away for a few days again.*

She waited a few days until he was in a good mood and then told him. Strangely he accepted it quite well, probably because it was a convent. So she prepared a small suitcase, and put all her college work together ready. She told the children it was just three days, and that they would be at school most of those days anyway. Gary agreed to come home early and also to collect Katy from her mother's each evening. It would not be long before Katy started school.

So the week before half term she set off for The Mount near Fareham. She had never been inside a convent before, and did not know what to expect. She parked the car in the car park, and made her way up to the big wooden door. She had expected it to be locked, but soon learnt it was always open wide. In the foyer were Ben and Jenny. They greeted each other. Ben jesting about where they were probably going to sleep on a cold floor. They all laughed, but no one knew what was in store for them at that point.

As people arrived, they were given a number and told to follow one of the nuns to their sleeping quarters. It would seem the back wing of The Mount was divided between upstairs and downstairs. Downstairs was for male visitors and upstairs for female visitors. Margaret was shown into a tiny cell which was very stark, on the first floor; just a small iron bedstead with a pillow and a couple of blankets, and a small table and upright chair. A very small slit window through which some light came into the room.

There was nowhere to put her clothes, so she left them in the case. She had been told the washroom was down the corridor, which she would have to share with her female colleagues. They all trooped downstairs and back into the main convent where coffee was being served in a large room where they would be tutored over the next three days. Various speakers would be arriving. One from Social Services to talk about Child Abuse, and a man would be coming who had been sexually abused himself also. A Psychologist would come and lecture them about psychological problems and how this affected families, and a project would be set for them too.

The food prepared by the nuns was rather bland but filling. A lot different from the meals they had at the hotel near Lyndhurst. During the day when they were not in lectures they used to see the nuns collecting produce from their smallholding, and eggs from the chickens. The nuns worked very hard.

During the first evening, after eating dinner the group split up, some went for a walk, and a few went into the games room, where you could play table tennis or whist. Andrea, Thora, Jenny, Dawn and Margaret sat talking about the day. Dawn suddenly said, 'Why don't we make up apple pie beds for the fellas?' Everyone stared at her, then started smiling, what a brilliant idea. One of the men on the course was a real misery, and it was decided that his bed would be the target. Jenny was sent off to keep the fellas busy, then armed with needle and cotton which someone produced, they stitched up Patrick's pyjamas, as well as folding the sheets in half. Lastly they unscrewed one of the bed legs and put the waste paper bin under the bed to hold it up. They also doctored Ben's bed, and put talcum powder in between the sheets.

With lots of giggling they returned to the lounge, where Jenny joined them. With everything achieved they made their way toward their upstairs dormitory. Everyone was giggling, and when the men were heard to make their way to their dormitory the ladies all stood on the stairs waiting for the result.

It was not long in coming. A loud crash, and loud shouts soon followed, the entire convent was in uproar. The ladies all dashed back to their cells. The following morning they learnt that the noise had woken the Padre, who wanted to know what was happening. The sister in charge of the dormitories, who was a real sweetie, had apparently had to pay penance for the disruption, because she should have ensured everything was in order. This made them all feel very bad for the rest of the day. The good sister spent the day in prayer and was not allowed any food. After that they all behaved themselves, and concentrated on their studies.

But it had been fun. Patrick never forgave them, but Ben thought it all good fun, as they knew he would.

The three days passed very quickly and soon they were off back home.

CHAPTER 19

The two new welfare officers were not as accommodating as Tom had been, and so at half term she had to fit in escort duties.

One of these was a girl called Emma who was blind, and was attending a school for the blind in South Wales. Emma was fourteen and a lovely girl. She was always happy and very chatty, and was brilliant at Braille. Margaret liked taking her to the Ysgol Peny Bont School at Bridgend. It was a long journey. From Harmsworth she had to travel along the M4 motorway and over the Severn Suspension Bridge and on into South Wales. It took Margaret most of the morning to get there. She would then stop for lunch in one of the motorway service stations on the return journey, and arrive home just before 5 o'clock.

She had other journeys to cope with as far away as Cornwall, Brighton and Pershore, but she quite liked driving, and she learnt a lot about the children she escorted, and the reasons why they could not be educated locally.

A job she detested was measuring distances with a pedometer to see if children qualified for bus passes. Junior age children had to live at least two miles from their school, and Secondary children at least three miles from their school. Walking was not one of her favourite pastimes, and it occupied a lot of her time.

Another Christmas dawned. Her mother and Ted came to Christmas dinner along with her brother John and his wife Elsa. She had made an effort with lots of little extras the children loved.

Besides the turkey with all the trimmings, she had cooked the Christmas pudding from her mother's recipe, which had pleased her mother, and made individual jellies and trifles as well as icing a cake. The Christmas tree groaned with the presents she had bought. Gary left things like that to her. In fact he left everything to her.

When she returned to work after Christmas she learnt the sad news that Mrs Kendrick had committed suicide. She had sent the children off to South Africa to her sister's, and in December she had seen her solicitor and ensured the will was in order. Mr Kendrick applied to the court to have the children returned, but the Judge decided he had to uphold the wishes of Mrs Kendrick, and after receiving a report from the authorities in South Arica made an order to that effect. Margaret felt sorry for Mr Kendrick, knowing he would now not see the children, unless he arranged to visit them in South Africa, but assured him that maybe when they were older they may choose to seek him out, and suggested that he write to them regularly.

Sarah had settled into her new school and was doing well. Margaret was pleased she had demanded a change of school for her. Peter was not doing so well, he seemed to have no interest in academic work, but got on well with the master who took the boys for a mechanics lesson. Peter certainly liked working with his hands, rather like his father. Gary was happiest tinkering with his car or washing it. He kept it in really good condition.

The house they rented from the local council was adequate for their needs, but was situated on a busy council estate. Margaret was not happy with the neighbourhood. She longed to live in a house of her own. With only paying rent she had managed to save quite a reasonable amount of money, which she put aside in the building society. She knew if Gary knew about it he would want to spend it. She took the opportunity whenever she could to try to find a suitable house for the family.

Anne changed jobs, and started work in the office of a coal merchants, situated in town. She had recently become very friendly with a young man who lived just along the road from them. Margaret felt she was seeing quite a lot of him. Gary warned her about going out with boys, emphasising she was still only a teenager.

Margaret decided the whole family needed a break and went to the local travel agents to see what offers were available. She wanted somewhere nice and warm. The spring weather in England was very cold. After much searching she found just what she was looking for. A week in Tenerife in the Canary Islands. All of them could go for a very reasonable amount. So she booked it. That evening she told Gary, who said he could do with a break. The factory where he worked was depressing and the job monotonous. He only enjoyed his extra job driving taxis for a friend of his.

So three weeks later they flew to Tenerife. It was magic, the weather was sunny and warm, when they first arrived. As soon as the plane landed and they disembarked they could feel the heat. They stayed in a two star hotel, nothing special, but Margaret did not have to cook as all the meals were 'all in'. They sunbathed and walked around Puerto de la Cruz, and on their third day took a coach trip up through the mountains, stopping on Mount Teide to see the volcano. The views were panoramic, but above the cloud base. They took lots of photographs and collected some lava to take home. They drove onto the south side of the island to Los Christianos where all the sand was black. It was a lovely day trip, which they all enjoyed. Unfortunately the weather deteriorated after that, and a lot of the time it was cold and windy, which was not very good for their suntans, and they were not able to frequent the swimming pool area of their hotel.

Anne was being chased by a waiter, who kept asking her to go out with him to a nightclub, which she declined.

All through the trip all she kept talking about was how much she missed Don her boyfriend. She could not wait to get back home. Everyone was enjoying themselves and Margaret began to think things were improving. Gary was nice to her and the children, even to Peter. He bought Margaret a crocodile handbag in the local market and gave the children money to spend too.

Anne wanted to buy a leather belt for Don, and went to a nearby shop. The male assistant told her that if she would go out with him on a date she could have the belt for nothing, but Anne was not swayed. She left the shop in a hurry, having paid for the belt.

The week soon passed, and then it was time to pack up and return to Harmsworth. Anne could not wait to get home. Margaret was soon back catching up on a pile of work, as well as her studies. Unbeknown to her Peter was missing days at school. He found Maths and English extremely hard and was opting out, telling the school he was unwell.

A letter from his year head informed them of the situation, and she had to visit his teacher and learn all the facts. There was nothing for it but to tell Gary. He hit the roof. He raced upstairs and Margaret could hear the beating Peter received, with Gary shouting at the boy. There was nothing Margaret could do. Peter had been wrong to skip school, especially with the sort of job she did; it did not look good. Fortunately Peter's school was not in her area. Peter was made to stay in his bedroom for a whole day, although she saw he received his meals when Gary was not about. Peter promised her he would not skip school anymore.

So Margaret was once more concentrating on her studies. The exams loomed large, and she knew she had six examinations to sit in June. She spent many hours when not working swotting. On the first day she sat her child care examination again as well as Sociology and the working of the Social Services Department. She was really nervous knowing she had failed child care the year before. On day two she took Central Government again as well as English, and on day three she took Local Government again as well as Social Policy. Six examinations in three days. By Thursday she felt quite ill and exhausted. By Friday she knew she was going down with influenza. She took to her bed, she felt so ill, and it was not until the following Tuesday that she felt like eating again. She decided to take the following few days off work and recuperate. By the following weekend she felt a lot better.

Anne wanted to work with horses, and a few weeks later she learnt that there was a job going as a stable maid just outside Harmsworth. It was a live-in job, and there was a caravan available for her to sleep in. She applied and was delighted when she was told she could have the job. Margaret was not so sure, she did not like the idea of Anne effectively leaving home, after all she was still only sixteen. A few months later Anne came home wearing an engagement ring.

'Don't you think it is a little soon to be getting engaged?' she asked Anne.

'But Mum, we love each other,' she replied.

'Well I think you ought to consider leaving it for a while, I presume you have not told your father yet?' The scared look on Anne's face told her everything.

'No I haven't, I thought you would tell him,' she said.

Margaret groaned inside. She would find a good time to tell him, but not just now. Although he had enjoyed the holiday he was back at the job he disliked so much, and was grumpy all the time.

Some weeks later Anne sheepishly told her mother that she was pregnant. Margaret told Gary that Anne was pregnant and also that she had recently become engaged to Don. She had never seen him so angry. He saw Anne as his little girl. She appeased him by saying that she had organised a meeting with Don's parents, Mr and Mrs Jenkins, for the following Saturday, and persuaded him to wait and see what was said.

Mr and Mrs Jenkins appeared concerned about the situation, but knew the problem lay with Don to resolve. Mr Jenkins was very pessimistic and suggested things would not last, after all they were both very young. Margaret left the room and went off to make some coffee, when she returned and after much discussion it was agreed that the couple wanted to get married. Anne would not hear of the baby being adopted, but it was agreed they would need some help financially, as well as somewhere to live.

Margaret offered to make a wedding dress and bridesmaids dresses, and bear the cost of the dresses and also the flowers. Don would pay for the licence and book the church, and Gary would be responsible for hiring a wedding car. Mr and Mrs Jenkins agreed to help with the catering and provide the drinks for the wedding reception. So the die was cast. A date was set for the wedding in November.

Some of the money Margaret had saved towards buying another house had to be spent on the wedding, but there was nothing she could do about this. She was still determined to move. It would just have to be postponed until she had saved more money.

At the beginning of August a brown envelope arrived addressed to her, postmarked Southampton. It was what she was dreading. She knew it was her examination results. She left the envelope sealed and put it behind an ornament on the mantelpiece. She had decided to open it later.

Margaret was called into a local comprehensive school by the headteacher and advised that two of the fourth year girls were pregnant, and asked what they could do about the situation. It was one thing for Anne to become pregnant at sixteen and working, but this was a totally different ball game. She said she would have to discuss this with her area supervisor. So later that day she took herself to the new area office in the town. She explained the situation to Sam Jackson, the Area Education Welfare Officer.

'Well Maggie I need to tell you that two other comprehensive schools have similar problems with girls who are pregnant. A decision needs to be made by the Education Officer as to what we do about it. By rights the girls should be excluded from school and have home tuition, but unfortunately that is expensive, and there are only limited resources of tutors.'

'I do not think these girls should lose out on their education, Mr Jackson, but it is a dilemma,' she said.

'Leave it with me and I will talk to the Area Education Officer as soon as he is free,' he told her. So she left the problem with him.

Two days later she was asked to report to the Area Education Officer's office. She had forgotten about her conversation with Mr Jackson until Mr Soper the Area Education Officer greeted her and having asked her to sit down brought up the subject. 'I am most concerned Mrs Pearce about the five girls we have within the area who are pregnant. I cannot allow them to remain in the school once they become five months pregnant, nor can I provide private tutors for all of them. Have you any suggestions?' he asked her.

'Well Mr Soper the only way forward as I see it is that these girls should be tutored together in a separate unit. That way we will only use one tutor and the girls would not be in school either,' she replied.

'What a wonderful idea,' he beamed at her, 'but where would we get a unit from?' he asked.

'Well may I suggest that one of the infant schools in my area is short of numbers, there are not enough children to fill the school. How about if we used two of the empty classrooms and turned it into a unit, where the girls could continue their education and after the babies are born could take their babies to the unit.'

'Mrs Pearce you are a marvel, that is brilliant, is there any chance you could set this up? I will arrange for limited funds to be available,' he continued to beam at her.

'Well I would like to visit other similar units I have heard about, both in Portsmouth and Bristol and make use of their ideas if I may,' she remarked.

'You most certainly can, and if you have any suggestions I would like to hear about them as soon as possible. Thank you so much for bringing this situation to my attention.' He stood up and came round his large desk with his hand outstretched, and shook her hand, before moving toward the door to open it for her. Margaret felt jubilant.

Within two days she had contacted other units and made arrangements to visit them as well as organising to go to London to the National Council for Unmarried Mothers, where she felt she would gain a lot of information and help, and she was right. Within the space of two weeks, she was able to arrange to see Mr Soper again, and armed with all the information she had gathered she advised him of her visits.

The units both in Portsmouth and Bristol worked on the basis that young unmarried mothers could leave school early, and continue their education in the units which had been set up. One teacher had overall responsibility for the running of the unit and ensured that guest speakers came in. These included Health Visitors and Midwives, to talk about the birth of a baby, and how to care for a baby, as well as someone from the DHSS to explain about benefits. A Paediatrician came in from the local hospital and a solicitor came to talk about legal matters.

In fact there was instruction on anything that was likely to affect the girls. Therapy sessions were arranged to help the girls sort out any problems they had, such as communicating with their parents and father of their child, and talking through whether they wanted their baby to be adopted or how they would cope if they kept the child. Mr Soper had suggested this might be a role she herself could play. Margaret knew she would like to be involved and felt the girls would appreciate the contact with her. She knew their circumstances and had already been involved giving them advice.

The main object of the unit was to allow any girl to finish her school studies and take their CSE examinations if they wished. If their parents were able to consider caring for the baby for a time, the girl could go back to school. But Margaret noted that at Portsmouth most girls who kept their babies would take them to the unit each day and care for them as well as keep up with their studies.

Mr Soper had listened carefully to the results of her search for information to help them set up a unit in Harmsworth. He had been most impressed, and told her when he attended the next meeting of Head Teachers for Secondary schools he would spread the word, as well as send a directive to each of these schools. In the meantime he would have the Adviser for part time tutors select a suitable female teacher for the project.

Within four weeks a teacher was found who was felt suitable, and the classrooms were transformed to accommodate the unit, which would have multi-functions. An academic room was set up with a small reference library, necessary writing books and equipment and comfy chairs. The other room was to be used for practical things and crafts. So by the end of the summer holidays everything was up and running. The unit started at the beginning of September with three girls, each within a few weeks of giving birth to their babies. Elizabeth Jones was to be the unit teacher who seemed very right for the role. A mother herself to teenage girls and very approachable. Margaret liked her straightaway. The unit would be open every morning from 9.30am - 12.30am Monday to Friday during term time.

CHAPTER 20

It was during the first week of the autumn term that Sarah came across the brown envelope behind the ornament on the mantelpiece.

'Mum what is this? It is addressed to you,' she held the letter towards Margaret.

'Oh I had forgotten all about that.' She stared at the envelope. Goodness it was her examination results. She stood transfixed, she could not bring herself to open it.

'What is wrong Mum?' Sarah demanded, concerned her mother had turned quite white. 'Oh nothing dear,' she continued to stand holding the envelope.

'It looks like the envelope you had last year with your examination results in,' Sarah stretched out her hand and took the envelope. Sure enough it had the college stamp on the envelope.

'I can't open it,' Margaret said, 'I do not want to know I have failed again.'

Sarah ever forceful, opened the letter and started to smile, 'Oh Mum, you are silly, this piece of paper says you have passed all six subjects.'

Margaret could not believe what her daughter was telling her, and took the piece of paper from her hand. Lo and behold it was right, she had passed all six examinations. She felt exalted. She had passed. She ran across the room to the telephone and dialled Andrea's number, she had to tell her friend. Andrea answered and Margaret told her the good news.

'I told you that you could do it, although it took its toll on you, but I knew you could do it. Wonderful, we must celebrate.'

So it was agreed that they would meet one lunch time and have a celebratory glass of wine. Margaret felt wonderful. All that hard work had paid off. When her wage slip came at the end of the month she realised she had received a substantial rise in pay. Gary was pleased about the extra money, but showed very little joy about her having passed her examinations. He made little remarks such as 'I didn't think you could do it.'

Margaret telephoned Sam Jackson, who it appeared already knew she had passed, and had known for a few weeks. He told her he was waiting for her to tell him. He congratulated her on the result as well as how well she had set up the unit for the pregnant schoolgirls. 'Maggie you are now a qualified Education Welfare Officer,' he told her.

She remembered the feelings she had as a child, longing to become a welfare officer. A lot of water had passed under the bridge since she had longed to care for people. She had worked hard to achieve success and she had done it.

Margaret met up with Andrea the following week in Winchester, where they had lunch. Andrea as always had a pot of tea but Margaret indulged in a small glass of white wine. They reminisced about the two years they had slogged and worked, but it had all paid off, they were both qualified. They promised each other to keep in touch even though they lived forty miles away.

******

Margaret started making the arrangements for Anne's wedding. The church was booked, and the flowers ordered. The local community hall was booked for the reception. Margaret true to her word, measured Anne and the chosen bridesmaids and started work on the dresses. It was a mammoth task, but it came as second nature to her to design and make the dresses. Everything was as Anne wanted it.

The wedding took p lace on the 25th November. It was a cold day but the watery sun shone for a while. The only real hiccup was that Anne had put on an extra inch round her waist and at the last minute Margaret had to alter the sash which was too tight, and sewed it together on Anne. There was no time to put new fasteners on it, but no one noticed. The wedding took place at St James Church in the town centre. It was a beautiful old Norman church, and the vicar knew all of her family. They had all been confirmed in that particular church. The wedding went very smoothly, but Margaret felt quite choked up during the service. Don looked very smart in his hired suit, and Anne seemed to glow. You could see she was very happy. The reception was a real family occasion, and relatives had come from miles around, both from Richmond in Surrey to Gillingham in Dorset. Mr Jenkins was roaring with laughter behind the makeshift bar, pouring drinks for everyone, absolutely in his element. Gary's mother attended as well as some of his brothers and Mrs Trent, Margaret's mother also attended as well as John and Elsa. It was a lovely party, but Margaret was exhausted by the end of the day, especially as they had to clear everything from the hall before they left just before midnight.

Anne's previous boss, who was a wealthy man, offered the couple a small caravan to live in temporarily, on a site he owned just outside of the town. Margaret did not like the idea of them living out in a lonely field, but it was agreed they would. It was not far from her mother's house, and Margaret knew Anne would visit her fairly often. Her mother was very fond of Anne.

Once more Christmas was upon them. It seemed strange to have fewer children at home. How she was going to miss Anne. She and Don were spending Christmas Day with Mr and Mrs Jenkins. To Margaret this was another loss in her life.

Gary became very irritable, and said he was bored with his job. He was not happy Margaret had invited her mother and her partner Ted for Christmas dinner again. Gary always felt inferior to her mother, which caused many an argument in the run up to Christmas. He constantly pestered her for sex, and Margaret learnt the art of having 'migraines'. She felt no love for him; it seemed to have died. She cared about him, after all he was the father of her four children, but she no longer respected him. If only Gary could understand her more. If only he could help her, instead of being so disagreeable all the time. If only he showed her some respect, and supported her efforts and her achievements, things might have been tolerable. After all she was earning good money, they were effectively out of debt. Each Sunday when she attended church she prayed for things to get better. Sometimes they improved a bit, but mainly everything made her terribly depressed. Was her whole life going to be like this?

She was glad when Christmas was over and all the decorations had been taken down. She spring cleaned the house, and started to look forward to the birth of her first grandchild, who was due at Easter.

The unit for pregnant schoolgirls was doing very well, and Margaret enjoyed her visits there where the girls learnt to knit and sew as well as keeping up their studies. A new entrant was starting at the unit during January, and Margaret had agreed to meet her boyfriend Greg who needed some advice. He had planned to leave school and go on to University once he had passed his A levels, but now the future looked bleak, he felt he would have to leave school and start a job to support the baby. He did not want Tanya his girlfriend to have an abortion, nor did he want the baby adopted. He wanted to marry her, but his parents had said he was too young to make such a decision. *How very wise of them* Margaret thought.

She went to see Tanya's parents who were still reeling from the shock, only recently having been told about the pregnancy. Margaret sat and listened to them, and let them talk about how angry and disappointed they were with Tanya, and more so with Greg, who they basically liked.

Margaret drew the meeting to a close by saying, 'I think we should all think about things for a short while and re-group in say, two weeks from now and try to make some solid plans for the future.' She made an appointment for the first week in February. Before then Tanya's parents would visit the unit and sit and talk with Greg's parents.

Peter was to leave school at Easter and was trying to find a suitable job. With no qualifications he had to find a job working with his hands. He went for two or three interviews, and at the end of February managed to secure one at EAS Motors as a trainee assistant behind the counter. It was a motor parts company. Peter knew a lot about cars, having helped Gary's mechanic and his father from time to time. He was to start after the schools broke up for the Easter holidays. So he had a job, not exactly what Margaret had wanted for him, and she hoped later on he would find something a little better.

Anne had grown to an enormous size, and during February endured getting around with difficulty. She was also experiencing a lot of backache. Margaret knew it would not be long before the baby was born. She dreaded to think of the baby living in the caravan, after all it was quite cold. There was just no space in the caravan.

The meeting with Greg and his parents was put off for two further weeks as Tanya went down with flu, so it was nearer the end of February when the two families came together and Margaret sat in with them to talk through the situation.

It seemed both sets of parents were of the same opinion. Firstly the baby would be born, and Greg and Tanya would complete their studies and with the help of the unit Tanya would sit her CSE examinations, in May. It was also decided that the couple should be given all the help possible to keep their baby. Tanya would move into Greg's parents very large house after the birth of the baby, and a further meeting would be set up between both their parents to look at the future and to see how everyone felt at that time. Greg still wanted to continue his studies and sit his exams about the same time as Tanya.

Margaret felt she could now leave the problem with these parents, they seemed very caring, and were being extremely supportive. She left, knowing she would see Tanya at the unit the following week.

As February turned into March, Anne was starting to get scared. Her back pains were getting worse and her GP decided she should go into the local maternity home. The pains got worse, but the baby did not come. Anne was in labour for three days and was very tired. The doctor made a decision, she must be transferred to the local hospital, and have a caesarean section operation immediately. Margaret went up to the hospital to sign the form, but found that Don had already signed it. Of course he was her husband. How silly of her.

Just a few hours later on the 6th March 1973 her first grandchild was born. Natalie a beautiful baby girl, weighing 6lbs 14 ounces. Gary was at work while all this was happening, and was cross that he was not allowed to see the child that evening. It was fathers only for visiting. But he was very chuffed and proud of Anne, and about becoming a grandfather himself.

CHAPTER 21

Anne left hospital just over a week later, and took Natalie to the caravan. Margaret was concerned the child would die of pneumonia in the damp conditions. The weather was cold and damp, and she made regular visits to the caravan to check on her young granddaughter. What a lovely child she was. After Gary's first euphoria about becoming a grandfather he rarely chose to visit Anne and the baby. Don was busy working every day except Sundays, when he took himself off to the pub to unwind. Anne saw little of him. But as Margaret had predicted, Anne spent a lot of her time with her grandmother.

Margaret had a lot of catching up to do, checking on all the clients on her case load. Although there were two other welfare officers now in Harmsworth and she had been told her workload would reduce, it did not feel like that. In fact it felt the exact opposite.

The unit for pregnant schoolgirls had expanded, and there were now six girls in the unit. She liked to call in and talk individually with each of the girls, and to discuss any problems which they had, and advise them of a course of action to take. She liked seeing the babies who now numbered three in the unit. It was great the girls could continue their education and take their examinations, so they did not lose out. She was also pleased that harsh decisions had been avoided as far as the babies were concerned. None of the girls wanted their babies adopted. The girls' parents gradually came round after the initial shock of learning their daughters were pregnant, and gave the young couples their support, allowing them to work out such things as where they would live, and whether the couple should marry eventually or how supportive were the natural fathers? Whether each or any one of them would pursue further education, or seek employment, and all the other questions about life and livelihood...

Her studies in Human Growth and Development, and Child Care helped a great deal and she was so grateful she had been allowed to take her recent course, and for Andrea's support and persuasion to keep going. It had all been worth it.

Margaret saved as much money as she could living on the local estate was getting to her. She desperately wanted to move, though she knew Gary preferred it where they were. But with Anne and Peter now working and Sarah attending a school in the town centre, it was an ideal time to move. Katy would be starting school in September. The only snag was that property prices had risen and it was hard to raise the deposit necessary on a reasonably priced property. Notwithstanding she did not want to live just anywhere. Margaret wanted to live in a more select district, after all she was earning good money and Gary's employment was sound, although he did not like working at the factory. She was trying not to rock the boat at present. Their relationship was tentative at times, and Gary was very sensitive to many things.

In July Peter upset his father over something fairly trivial. The whole incident blew up out of all proportion. They were both facing each other in the kitchen. Gary was shouting at Peter, pointing his finger at the boy, stressing in no uncertain terms he would not tolerate his behaviour much more. Suddenly Peter swung his fist at his father's face and hit him right on the nose, causing his nose to bleed. Gary taken aback for a second, soon recovered and lashed out at Peter, and before she knew it they were having a fist fight; each glaring at each other. It ended with Gary screaming at Peter telling him to get out and never come back. Peter ran out of the back door.

Gary turned to her, 'Never let that boy back in this house,' he shouted at her. 'No boy of mine would never have hit me like that.'

She stood mortified. Tears welled in her eyes. 'Why didn't Gary love Peter? He was his son, he could never dispute it, Peter looked so like his father.' The problem had always been that Peter was of a stocky build and not slim like Gary. Gary did not understand genes and how features in a child often stemmed from a different generation. What was she to do? Of course Peter had to come back home.

She busied herself clearing up the kitchen. There was blood on the floor. The household became very quiet, and she wondered where Peter had gone.

It started to get dark, she sat fretting, whilst Gary watched the television. Just after nine o'clock the telephone rang. She got up and answered it. It was Peter.

'Mum I want to come home,' he said.

'Where are you Peter?' she asked him.

'I am at Neil's flat, but I cannot stay here. Is Dad still angry?' he asked.

'I am afraid so, though he has calmed down,' she told him. 'I suggest you come home, I'll go and talk to him.' She replaced the receiver. She dreaded talking with Gary but it must be done. She braced herself and went into the lounge.

'Gary I must talk with you,' she started.

'What about?' he demanded.

'About Peter, and before you say anything let me tell you, you were in the wrong earlier and Peter was right. I accept he should never have hit you, but you goaded him. Peter is still under sixteen and therefore he has a right to stay here under our protection. I want him to come home.' She stood her ground, defying him.

He did not answer. She turned on her heels and went back to the telephone and dialled Neil's number. When she spoke again to Peter she told him to come back home.

At half past ten Peter arrived. You could tell he was wary, but she told him to go up to bed.

Gary came out of the lounge and brushed past Peter never saying a word, just glaring at the lad. Peter rushed up the stairs. Nothing further was said. Margaret heaved a sigh of relief. *I cannot stand much more of this* she thought.

Gary sulked for five days. Everyone suffered. The children all spoke in whispers, and Peter only came home to sleep, he mainly stayed at his friend's flat after work. Neil's mother was very kind. She was a single parent and spoilt Neil a lot. But she was kind to Peter too, and told him it would all blow over shortly.

Although it did, things between father and son remained strained for some while.

That same week Charlie their dog became ill and Margaret took her to the vets. He showed her there was a lump on her abdomen. Charlie underwent an X-ray and scan. The kindly vet explained that he could remove the growth, but there were strong indications that the growth was malignant and would spread. Margaret opted for the operation, and left the dog there. She knew the children would be devastated if they lost Charlie, she decided to give her a chance of survival, but came away from the vets in tears.

The following day she collected Charlie, who was still dopey. She had taken the girls with her and they were pleased Charlie seemed all right. The vet however told Margaret it was only a matter of time. He had found traces of malignancy elsewhere. A month later Charlie died. Everyone was distraught even Gary.

CHAPTER 22

The summer of 1973 was mainly dry and sunny. Margaret spent spare moments sitting in the garden trying to get a tan, and spending time reflecting. She thought back to when she left school and all the promise of a good life ahead of her. She had certainly attained her ambition to be a welfare officer, and she had managed to go to college with the help of the County Council. It had been hard work, but she had achievements under her belt. She was a qualified welfare officer.

Marriage had been an uphill struggle, and nothing like the romantic dream she had thought it would be. There was no romance, and very little love. It was a day to day struggle with money, and the family interactions were a daily challenge, especially her relationship with Gary.

What could she do to change things, life could not continue in the same vein, she knew that much of the time she was crying inside. The children were suffering as the arguments continued. She and Gary had different needs.

She had never caught up financially since Anne's wedding, the money she had borrowed from her savings had not been replaced. There was not enough money for the deposit on a different house. She longed to leave the area they lived in.

Since the wedding last November she had missed Anne, although she was delighted with her beautiful granddaughter and took every opportunity to visit her. She was a beautiful baby, and Margaret adored her. There was nothing she liked better than to hold her and watch her smile when she talked to the child.

Her job was going well and she still found it very rewarding, although there were times when she wished she were a Social Worker. Many of her interesting cases she had to hand over to Social Services because they came under the umbrella of that department. She knew that she would have to go to college and train for years to become a social worker, and that she stood little chance of achieving this ambition.

The relationship between Gary and Peter was very fraught. Gary appeared jealous of the boy. They were certainly not the best of friends, but enjoyed similar interests. Cars and motorbikes were top of their list, whether it was the family cars or watching motor sports on the television.

Her relationship with her mother had improved over the years, especially since her mother had moved to the local area. She had been most helpful in minding Katy whilst Margaret had worked, and Margaret loved the times she could sit and talk with her mother's partner Ted, who always listened to her and occasionally offered advice.

Sarah was a quiet child and very studious. She was also very musical and was doing well at her piano lessons. Margaret had always found the money for her lessons, even though at times it had been hard. Margaret missed not playing the piano herself, but it had always started arguments between herself and Gary. If she lifted the lid of the piano, or started to play, he quite often put the television on and drowned her out. He did not seem to mind Sarah practising. She concluded he was a strange person at times.

Now she had Katy starting school within a few weeks at the local infant school. It would be a weight off her mind as the child would be at school all day and she could get on with her work.

Margaret worried every day and many nights about Anne and her baby granddaughter. She had recently driven to the caravan and was shocked to see rats running around. Anne told her they were always there but did not come into the caravan, but she would not put the baby outside in her pram, she usually walked to her grandmother's bungalow with the pram and put Natalie in the garden there for her afternoon sleep.

She decided to write to the local housing department at the council, stressing there was an urgent need to house Anne and Don because of their situation, she also took the opportunity to mention the rats she had seen, and that she felt that the Environmental Health Department should be asked to assess the situation.

Within a week Anne was contacted by the housing department offering her one of the newly built terraced houses on the northern fringe of the town, one was available but it was number 13. Anne was not overly superstitious and whooped with joy, and Margaret was happy that the family were moving out of that awful caravan. So two weeks later Margaret and Gary helped them move their things into the completed house.

The summer holidays seemed long, as they had decided just to take a few days out, and not go away. The previous occasions with the caravan were never to be repeated. It was so hot especially late August. Margaret bought some winter dresses for Katy to start school in, but during the first week of term, regretted this as poor Katy would come out of school pouring with perspiration and complaining of being too hot. So Margaret ran up a couple of gingham school dresses for her on the sewing machine.

One afternoon she came in from work and made a cup of tea and took it out into the garden. While she sat there she decided she would look around for another house, and start saving in earnest.

Peter was having problems at work and also needed to earn more money. He desperately wanted to buy a motorbike. His friend Neil was working for a local company, office cleaning, but it paid well. So Peter applied and was given a job working with Neil. Poor Peter he never had any money. He was always borrowing money from her and paying her back on his next pay day. The girls used to sing him the Abba song 'Money Money Money, it's a Rich Man's World'. Margaret felt sorry for him, but there was no way she could help him.

Her Area Manager advised her that the Education Welfare Certificate was being replaced by the CQSW (Certificate of Qualification in Social Work) and that she would need to go on another course to get the extra qualification. *Oh Lord,* she thought, *all that learning and preparation for examinations all over again.*

Peter bought his motorbike with the aid of a hire purchase agreement, and Margaret agreed to be guarantor. She knew his outgoings were tight, but if he was careful he could just do it. She knew he wanted the bike so badly, and his friend Neil had a motorbike. Gary was not pleased, and argued with her about the stupidity of letting him have a bike before he had saved money for it. *He's a fine person to talk,* she thought. If Gary wanted something, he would get it and leave her to pay for it.

In October the weather started to deteriorate. They were well and truly into autumn. Margaret loved this time of year when all the leaves changed colour, with different hues of gold and copper tones, but she hated it when all the leaves fell from the trees and knew there was only winter to look forward to. How she hated the cold, dark days and nights the constant rain, and the threat of snow and ice.

Christmas came and went like any other and in the early spring of 1974 she was advised her name had been put forward for the CQSW course at Southampton. She decided not to tell Gary for the time being. The course did not start until September.

She had started looking at houses in the south of the town, but came across difficulties. Firstly they were very expensive, and secondly Gary complained people in that area were too stuck up, he did not want to live there. *But I want to* she thought, *why can't I live where I want to?* But she was no nearer to resolving the situation.

Peter had decided he wanted to join the army, and talked her into going with him to the army recruitment centre in the town. The sergeant, who was a big man, slapped Peter on the back and told him he would have to complete a test first, and to go back the following day and sit the test. He wanted to go in the REME but the results of the test were not good enough. He was told he could join the Hampshire Regiment and do his basic training in Yorkshire. He decided that was what he wanted to do. She had such mixed feelings, but Gary said it would do him good. So some weeks later, Margaret said farewell to her son.

CHAPTER 23

With both Anne and Peter not living at home, the house seemed empty. Sarah was always studying and at weekends she often met up with a few friends. Katy was a very lively child and Margaret was often grateful for her company.

Gary spent three evenings a week driving taxis until nearly midnight. Although she had no studying to do, she busied herself with reports for head office as well as the inevitable court reports.

There seemed to be an increase in truancy in the area and she spent many hours combing the town centre, checking all the places children congregated, such as caféterias, the local cinema and the large park behind the council building.

Sam Jackson the Senior Education Officer informed her he had put her name forward for the CQSW course which would probably start in September. She thanked him and decided now she had more free time and less commitments at home she would certainly take up the opportunity.

It was in May that Peter arrived home from his camp. He had a week's leave before being posted. He was scared this would involve active service abroad. He appeared to get on well with Gary and the week flew by. He told Margaret that he had enjoyed some of the training, but did not like the sergeant major, who often sought him out and meted out punishments for misdemeanours. He did not like the food and his bed was not very comfortable. At the end of the week he packed his case and she took him to the railway station to catch his train. She said a weepy goodbye and drove on to one of the comprehensive schools. She had received a phone call from a year head about a boy of 13 years of age, and agreed to talk with him about the boy's situation.

Bill Grimes was always very interested in the pupils under him, and took a great deal of trouble to sort out any problems they had.

He told Margaret about Richard who lived quite near the school with his mother who was a single person. His father had died suddenly about two years ago.

'Maggie we find that Richard is a very gifted boy. As well as being very studious, he loves music and plays the violin in the school orchestra,' he told her. 'He really needs a private music teacher, or a scholarship to a school of music, but unfortunately Mrs Brown his mother has no way of helping, have you any ideas?' he asked.

She thought for a minute, and then she had a brainwave. There was a school at Petersfield called Bedales who took boys and girls where music was studied. 'I think I have an idea, which I will follow up,' she told Bill, 'and I will talk to the boy's mother, as it would mean he would be away from home during term time.'

'Thanks Maggie, let me know if you hear anything,' he said as he went off to join his class.

That afternoon she went to see Mrs Brown. She lived in one of the council houses nearby, and Margaret knew that she worked part time in the mornings at a local newsagents. Richard had applied to her recently for a work permit to do a paper round in the mornings before he went to school.

Mrs Brown was surprised to see her when she called, and invited her in. Over a cup of tea Margaret tested the water about her feelings regarding Richard being put forward for a scholarship to Bedales. She saw Mrs Brown looking troubled, and soon explained how much she would miss Richard if he were away for much of the term as she would then be on her own. Margaret understood this.

'You see I rely on Richard a lot, and I would miss cooking his dinner, and in the evenings I would have no one to talk to,' she sat considering the opportunity it would be for Richard. She finally said if he wanted to be considered she would not stand in his way. 'How will I be able to afford the uniform, and items he will need?' she asked. Margaret assured her that the Education Department would provide him with a clothing grant and anything else he needed she would acquire somehow.

So the following morning she returned to see Bill Grimes and explained Mrs Brown was prepared to let Richard go if he passed the scholarship. 'Yippee!' he said, 'I will talk to Richard about the possibility.'

She returned home for lunch, and while eating her sandwich the telephone rang. It was Peter. He told her he was still at the station, and that he had missed his train. She could not believe this, she had taken him in plenty of time before the train left.

She picked up her car keys and headed for the railway station. There stood Peter with his suitcase. He climbed into the car and sat in silence all the way home. She made a cup of coffee for him and then he told her he could not face going back. 'But Peter you will be AWOL and they will come and pick you up.' She beseeched him.

'I know,' he wailed. 'But I do not want to go back, I want to leave the army, I hate it.' She could see the tears in his eyes.

'Peter you have to go back,' she told him. 'If you want to leave the army you must see your commanding officer and advise him that under the terms of your entry, you could apply within six months to leave, but you must go back.' She could feel how unhappy he was about the prospect of returning to camp.

She got up, 'I will telephone the guard house and advise them that you have missed your train and will be on the train tomorrow.' He nodded in agreement, and went upstairs to his room.

The following day she saw him off, and went onto the platform with him to ensure he caught the train, and advised him what to do on his return to camp. She then set off to see Bill Grimes again, when she learnt that Richard could sit the scholarship exam in two weeks time.

She made enquiries about a possible grant from the school trust fund, and she knew if Richard was offered a place there were many things he would need beside the basic uniform, including a violin, which he did not possess.

She contacted Bedales College and was advised there was a place available for Richard in Dunhurst Junior House if he passed the scholarship. She felt elated. It was an unusual part of her job, and something she had never had to do before, but very pleasurable. She kept her fingers crossed that Richard would do well with his exams.

She wondered whether her own name had gone forward for the course at Southampton which was due to start in September. She had heard nothing since Sam Jackson had mentioned it. There had been no point mentioning it to Gary until she was sure it was on the cards.

It was three weeks before she heard from Bill Grimes, who advised her that Richard had passed the scholarship. *Hurrah* she thought. Well done Richard.

She called to see his mother, who looked delighted that her son had done so well. Gone was the doubts about being alone. She explained that the grant for clothing would only cover the basic uniform, but that she would apply to the school trust to enable them to buy all the items that he would require including his own violin. She knew they were expensive, but she was determined to send him off with everything he needed.

She contacted the trust and was told the matter would be placed on the agenda for the next monthly meeting. Richard's place was available for him in September.

Three weeks later she learnt that a very handsome sum of money had been placed at her disposal to kit out Richard for his entrance to Bedales. She knew a lot about the piano but nothing about violins. She sought out Bill Grimes and asked for his help. Within the space of a few weeks he had located an instrument he felt was most suitable for the boy. Gosh it was expensive, but she had sufficient funds to pay for it.

She met Richard at school one day and explained the violin was now available for him and that she would be taking him to Bedales College the second week of September. He looked nervous, but pleased he was going to study music which he loved.

She learnt from Sam Jackson that her own placement for the CQSW course was now listed for September 1975. Apparently there were so many people who wanted to acquire the certificate now that the Education Welfare Certificate had been upgraded that there was a shortage of places to go round. *Ah well* she thought *that gives me a further year to work hard within the area and hopefully look for another house.* She was determined to move.

Sarah and Katy had been pestering her for quite some time to get another dog. Living on the council estate and living in such a tall house, it was not really appropriate. The girls had an ally with Anne who adored animals and who had tried to bring dogs home when she worked at the veterinary clinic.

One day Sarah came rushing into the kitchen and showed her mother a picture of a dog in the local newspaper. It looked like a large spaniel. 'Oh mum this dog needs a good home,' she pleaded. 'Can we have her? She looks so sad and the article says they have tried in vain to find a home for her. They may have to put her down.'

Margaret was swayed. The dog looked very sad and appealing, and she had always wanted a dog, but what with the upkeep and her being out of the house all day, it had never been practical. 'I don't know,' she faltered, which was fatal. Sarah was joined by Katy who looked up at her mother and said, 'Oh please can we go and look at her. Please?'

'I'll think about it,' she replied, and turned to continue preparing the dinner. *Oh Lord* she thought *could she possibly manage a dog?* She decided to ask Gary that evening.

She was really surprised when she mentioned it to him, that he thought it was a good idea, and suggested they went to see the dog at the weekend. So the following day she rang the number and offered to take a look at the dog. The woman on the end of the line seemed quite jubilant, and told Margaret where the dog was placed, somewhere out in the countryside with 'foster parents'.

So on the Saturday, they drove out to a small village in Berkshire. Sadie the dog was huge, a cross between a Spaniel and a St Bernard. The lady looking after her explained she was a clumber spaniel, who had a lovely nature, and hoped they could find a home for her before they had to admit defeat and have her put down. Sadie continually wagged her tail and loved the girls stroking her. 'Oh please Mummy can we have her?' Katy pleaded.

Margaret despaired. 'You will have to ask your father,' she eventually said.

Surely Gary could see this dog was too big. But to her surprise he loved the dog, and was talking to the woman's husband about what she was fed on. So it was no surprise to her some half an hour later that they set off back home with the dog. Sadie whined. She was in the back seat but her head over the front seats. They eventually opened the back window and Sadie put her head out of the window and continued to whine.

When they arrived home Sadie could not settle, and wandered around the house whining. Eventually Margaret found an old teddy bear belonging to one of the children and an old blanket and made up a bed for her. She eventually settled, until Margaret was woken about 3am with the dog scratching the kitchen door and whining. She went downstairs and sat with the dog and eventually fell asleep on a chair, but the dog finally settled, and when she woke up she found Sadie was sitting at her feet with her head nestling on her lap, looking up at her with such soulful eyes. Margaret's heart melted. The day before she had threatened the girls that the dog had to go back, but looking at her now she knew they would keep her.

It gave her great pleasure to take Richard to Bedales in the September and she was most impressed with all the college facilities. She also realised that many of the 'children' there came from well appointed homes and some brought their own ponies, and many luxury items to the college. She hoped Richard did not feel threatened, or that he would gain an inferiority complex about his poor background. She hoped he would benefit from what the college was offering him, a chance to study music and possibly gain a career in the music world, which she knew he wanted more than anything.

She received a letter from Peter to say when he had returned to camp a few weeks ago, he had been confined to barracks for 72 hours as a punishment for missing his train. His sergeant major had not been best pleased with his explanation, and was on his back all the time. He had been able to arrange to see the commanding officer last week, and advised him he did not feel a career in the army was for him. The officer had tried to talk him into alternatives with the service, but Peter told her he had stood his ground and requested consideration was given to him returning to Harmsworth. The officer had advised him that he would be put forward for discharge, and he would not have to buy himself out of the service as he had joined on the proviso that he gave it a six month trial.

It was another two weeks before she heard from him again to say he had been granted discharge and would be on his way home the following Friday afternoon. Margaret heaved a sigh of relief. She knew Peter had been most reluctant to go back to Yorkshire, and glad he would be home soon. She arranged to meet him at the local station on Friday evening. Gary was not impressed. Having done his own National Service for two years, and had to stick it out, he felt Peter was a bit of a wimp to give in so soon.

She waited at the station for a long time as the train was late, but eventually it pulled into the station. She saw Peter striding along and she ran to meet him. She hugged him and they walked arm in arm towards her car. Now all he had to do was find a job.

In the next few months she started searching in earnest for a house in the south of town, but it was early January before she found the house she wanted and at the right price. She discovered a three bedroomed semi detached house in a small close. It had a nice garden and a garage and the owners wanted to move as quickly as possible so that they did not lose the cottage they wanted to buy in Redruth in Cornwall. She made an offer and they accepted it.

She was quite excited and then told Gary about it. He was not impressed. He could not see why they needed to move. He argued with her for days, but eventually agreed to go and see the house she had made an offer on. When he saw it he agreed it was very nice and would accommodate their depleted family quite well. She felt elated, how she longed to leave their present house. It was not the house so much as the location. It was so noisy on the estate that they lived, and many of the neighbours left much to be desired, and some of them resented the fact she worked for the council. She had called on many of the houses because of truancy, or the family circumstances and they did not treat her with respect.

It took some weeks to secure a mortgage and to sort out all the legalities but eventually by March everything was in order. In April they moved house.

Having lived for some years in such a large house it took a bit of getting used to living in a smaller house, but they had plenty of furnishings, and soon the new house in Spring Close looked very nice. It had been easy to decorate, and the garden although much bigger, was mainly laid to lawn, with flowerbeds already planted. The bottom of the garden Margaret turned into a vegetable patch, so that she could grow a few vegetables. She was in her element. Her salary coped with the new mortgage and she felt happy for the first time for ages. If only her relationship with Gary could improve. She had planned another holiday, but unfortunately her savings would only stretch so far, so the holiday had to be abandoned.

CHAPTER 24

Margaret loved the new house, and also her neighbours. There were only twelve houses in the close, and she soon knew this was the sort of area she wanted to live. People were friendly and Katy soon made friends with a few girls from the local school. Katy had had to change schools as it was too far to her previous one, but Sarah caught a bus into town, just the same, just coming from a different direction.

The house backed onto fields. Margaret enjoyed a peaceful walk along the pathways. She would often take Sadie the dog with her for company. Sadie had settled down, and the girls loved her.

They often enjoyed dressing her up. Sadie would patiently sit while they put a cardigan on her and a headscarf. She would sit dribbling knowing the girls would reward her with some of their sweets. She was adorable and when she had enough of their playing with her, she would wander into the kitchen to seek Margaret out, who would take instant pity on her, and remove the clothing. But the dog loved it really.

Not long after moving house, Sam Jackson asked her to visit a boy called Tom Willis who lived in the next road to her. He was 14 years of age and suffering from leukaemia. He was currently undergoing extensive treatment and his parents had requested that he continued with his schooling, but needed transport to school. He only attended on two days a week, as the treatment left him fairly drained.

The school he attended was her main comprehensive school, and after meeting him and his parents, she offered to take him to school herself on those two mornings. She liked Tom. She could always tell when he was having a bad day, and would advise the school staff accordingly. She had been taking him for some six weeks when his mother telephoned her and said that Tom was not well enough to go one day.

Within a week he had died. Margaret felt quite bereft, she had liked Tom and his pleasant nature. A few days after his funeral she went to see his parents and empathised with them. She stayed for some while, allowing them to talk about the boy and how much they were going to miss him. It would be some time for them to come to terms with their loss. She herself would miss him too, he had been such a happy go lucky character.

During the summer months a local carnival was held, when Harmsworth staged various activities, ie dog shows, fashion shows, bingo games, but the highlight was the Carnival Parade which was always held on the Thursday during that week. The townspeople would decorate large floats and nearly everyone would be involved.

Margaret despaired as this also heralded the arrival of a fair which was situated near the back of the large town park. Children often skipped school when the fair was in town, and she spent a lot of her time visiting the fair during the day time and taking children back to school, and notifying their parents. After the fair left town there was always at least one girl who was pregnant. The girls often followed the boys working on the fair rides. They seemed to hero worship them. So quite often within a few short months another girl would join her pregnant schoolgirls group.

Sam Jackson called her to his office in July and advised her that a place was available for her on the CQSW course starting in September. 'Fine,' she told him, 'I want to do that course, it was sad the previous course was disbanded and my certificate does not qualify me as a welfare officer, but this certificate will ensure I become a social worker, and that is what I want to do.'

That night she told Gary about the course. He did not seem to have any objections as she would be doing day release each week just as she had before. She contacted

Anthea who told her she was also going on the course, and so was Jenny and Dawn, but Anthea knew she would not be able to take the final third year. Margaret was not sure if she could either, she would have to apply to a university for Phase 3 and be seconded. It was a gamble.

So in September 1975 she started College at Southampton once more going each Friday for the day. Now the class would be studying different subjects as well as some she had previously studied. Human growth and Development, and Child Care she was familiar with. Children's law, and how it affected the Social Services Department as well as Education. They also studied Psychology and Sociology, which Margaret found most interesting. They looked at Fostering and Adoption, and the work of the courts really appealed to her. She had taken many cases before the juvenile court for truancy, and social problems, but most of them had then been passed over to Social Services and she very rarely knew the total outcome of them. The law was changing, and Education Welfare Officers were to be given more powers. Firstly if they applied for a Supervision Order or a Care Order because of Truancy or bad behaviour, the orders would be made so that EWO's would supervise those children and they would not be passed to Social Services. She would attend Case conferences for children alleged to have been abused by their parents or others, and remain involved. She liked what she heard, and studied diligently in her spare time.

She tried to spend as much time as she could with the children, and also with Gary. He still resented her involvement on the course, and to punish her he spent more of his evenings driving taxis. Margaret did not really mind, she realised that she and Gary were moving further and further apart.

She had loved Gary since she was fifteen years of age, she had dreamt of a happy life with him. He did not understand her, and his upbringing, which had been so different from her own did not help. He felt the world owed him a living, and wanted only to rent a house and live from week to week. She on the other hand wanted a house she could call her own, and be able to save money and be secure. They were poles apart.

If only Gary would put his arms around her and say he loved her from time to time she felt she would cope. But he didn't. It was just sex and more sex, often when she was feeling tired. She felt unloved and unhappy. She gained a great deal of happiness from watching the children grow up and being involved in their situations as well as the satisfaction she gained from her job.

The first term went by very quickly, and just after the Christmas holidays she started to suspect that Gary was seeing someone else. Just her sixth sense. He would go out in the evening as though he were going to drive taxis, but he would be humming to himself and he would be home earlier than usual. Another taxi driver who called at the house to give him a message kept making smirky comments. A lady rang from time to time asking for Gary.

On one occasion Margaret asked this woman who she was, and she told Margaret to tell him it was Mrs Archer trying to contact him. When she mentioned it to Gary, he dismissed it instantly, as though he did not know who she was. Then one day in March they were having a blazing row because his dinner was not ready in time, that he shouted at her, 'Jane Archer is much nicer than you' then stopped in his tracks. Stunned, Margaret asked, 'Who is Jane Archer Gary?'

'No one,' he replied, 'just someone I know.' He turned on his heel and ran up the stairs. She had lots of unanswered questions, but she knew he had clammed up. Yes she knew he was seeing someone else.

The following day while she was checking the registers at one of the local schools, one of the taxi drivers, Tony Gilby, who knew Gary well, called at the school office to pick up a fare. The secretary asked him to wait and said she would locate whoever had ordered the taxi.

Margaret smiled at Tony. He recognised her and smiled back before coming over to talk to her. She decided she would ask him about Gary. 'Gary worked late last night,' she ventured, 'were you all busy?' she asked him.

'Not especially, and to be honest between 9pm and 10pm we were mainly sitting on the taxi rank,' he told her.

'Oh I see, I gained the impression you were,' she looked away.

'Well we were busy after 10pm with people leaving the pubs and cinema. We were glad then that Gary was back. Did he pop home for an hour or so?'

'Why do you ask?' she questioned.

'Well Gary took his regular fare Mrs Archer home from town about half past eight as he usually does, somewhere out your side of town, and was not back until the rush at 10pm.'

'Well actually Tony, I did not see Gary, he left home at half past six as usual and I have not seen him since. He was up at half past six this morning and off to work.'

He looked round as someone entered the foyer. His fare had arrived, and he left, waving goodbye to her.

So Gary is seeing Mrs Archer, she thought. She wondered how long it had been going on. How convenient to see one of his taxi clients, and in working time. Was he at work every evening he went out to drive taxis? He was certainly working more evenings than he had before they moved house.

The picture was gradually fitting together. Was that what the other driver had been smirking about the other day? Was she the only one not to know? Was that why Gary was angry because the dinner had not been ready at half past five the day before?

Tears welled in her eyes. She had been loyal to him for over twenty years. The times he had accused her of seeing someone else, which was all in his jealous mind. She would never forgive him for this, any love she still felt for him seemed to ebb away. She had to keep things going for the sake of the children, but in her heart she knew she did not love him any more.

She knew she had to ensure she earn good money, and so she would throw herself into her studies, but once qualified she would reassess the situation. The course would last two years, which would give time for Sarah to finish her O Levels and leave school next year. Sarah was already determined she would probably go on to college for a secretarial course, and Katy would be another two years older. She had a lot to think about.

CHAPTER 25

Sarah passed her mock examinations with flying colours. She had just one more year before taking her O Levels and then she would move on to the local college and take a secretarial course. Margaret was quite confident she would do just that.

Katy appeared to like her new school and had a friend called Jacqueline who she met at her new school, and they became inseparable.

Margaret's course was going well at Southampton. They were currently studying mental health. The tutor took them on day trips to Knowle Mental Hospital near Fareham as well as to Netley where they met staff and patients. Margaret found mental health a little frightening, but knew it was a subject she had to do and do well.

Peter found himself a job. There was not a lot of work about, but he was lucky enough to be taken on at Décor Market, a wallpaper and paint shop as a store floor salesman. He did not like working a six day week, but he quite liked the job, and earned a reasonable wage, enough to keep up the payments on his motorbike, and go out with his friend Neil and his girlfriend Kathy. He was to keep this job for eighteen months before moving in 1977 to a Builders Merchants as a warehouseman, where he would learn all about plumbing and heating, and eventually to take charge of that department.

Sarah finally completed her schooling and applied for a place at college, and within a few weeks of applying, learnt she had been accepted, to start in September. Her children were all growing fast and gradually leaving the nest. It would be sometime before Katy reached this stage, and then there would just be her and Gary. She found the situation galling. There were many disagreements, and angry sessions which left her cold. She hated it when Gary was in a bad mood, and would shout at her and point his finger into her face, or poking her arm. She questioned herself over and over again. Was there any love left in their relationship? Could it be salvaged? Why was Gary so possessive? Why was he seeing someone else? Was he seeing someone else or was he just trying to frighten her? What would happen if she gave up her job and stayed at home, would it make any difference? She did not think so, she would just be lonely, and they would have little money to live on. There would just be more rows about money, especially since Gary had taken to buying a lot of electrical gadgets. There were so many offers in the shops, have now pay later. But he never paid now or later, it was always left to her to pay up for the things he bought.

No she must continue with her course, and keep praying when she went to Church that things would get better somehow. Her hopes and fears were always with her.

She studied hard and on her working days threw herself into her job. Christmas loomed ahead. Anne and Don were divided where to spend Christmas, and Peter told her that on Christmas Day he was spending the day at his girlfriend's house. He was seeing more and more of Kathy. He sometimes stayed at her house at weekends. Kathy had three brothers, and Peter liked being with them. She felt they had encouraged him to join the army, as two of Kathy's brothers were in the Royal Hampshire Regiment, and liked the life.

So Christmas was going to be a rather quiet affair. She decided to invite her brother John and his wife over, as well as her mother and partner Ted. This threw Gary into a paddy.

'Why have we got to have all of them here?' he shouted at her.

'Because I want them here, no doubt you will be out much of the time, earning double time on the taxis, I do not want to spend Christmas on my own,' she replied.

'Well you will have Sarah and Katy here,' he retorted.

'Well I want to have my family here and the girls will appreciate the company, she rounded on him. 'Don't you think that for once you could take some time off and let us enjoy some time together?'

'I would rather talk with the taxi customers than your family,' he shouted back.

She could hold it no longer. 'I suppose you will be taking Jane Archer home or calling on her?' Tears stung her eyes. She turned and went out through the back door into the garden. He did not reply or follow her. Her remarks had hit home.

She would organise Christmas, and hopefully everyone would enjoy themselves, with or without Gary.

The following year she once more flung herself into her studies, there was only a few months before Phase 1 and 2 of her course would come to an end, and she had essays to write, and projects to do. After that it would be in the lap of the gods. She would have to put her name forward to be seconded to university. She would see Sam Jackson shortly, she knew he favoured her completing the three phases of the course. He was such a kind man, and was a fatherly figure she looked up to. She laughed to herself that Gary had once accused her of having an affair with him, after all Sam was about to retire.

In May Sam called her into the office, and advised her that her name had been put forward to the County Council but she was not being offered a secondment by the department. It was a mortal blow, what would she do now? She could not afford to pay for the course herself. She returned home at lunchtime, feeling absolutely devastated. There was no one home. She rushed upstairs and threw herself on the bed and cried. It was sometime before she pulled herself together and went and washed her face. It looked a blotchy red mess, but she had house visits to do that afternoon. She creamed her face, and powdered it well, before leaving home to call on clients.

Margaret was deeply depressed and very quiet for the next two weeks, but a phone call from Andrea early one afternoon lifted her spirits. 'Maggie have you seen the Hampshire Chronicle?' she asked.

'No, why?' she asked her friend.

'Well on page five there is an advert where Social Services are offering Bursaries for Phase 3 of our course, so that people can take their final year. I thought of you straightaway, I think you should apply.'

'Well thanks Andrea I will go and buy the paper straightaway.' She put the phone down, picked up her car keys and drove to the nearest paper shop, where she bought the paper. She sat in her car and opened it to page five, where Andrea had indicated. Sure enough the department were offering to pay all college fees and a book allowance, plus a lodgings allowance. She tore out the article, and went into the nearest school and rang the number asking for an application form.

Within a week the form arrived. She filled it in and sent it off straightaway. She knew she may not get it, she worked for a different department, but it was her only hope.

Three weeks later she received a letter which requested she went to Winchester, and gave the time and place, where she would be interviewed by three different people. So far so good, she thought, though she felt very nervous about it. She disliked interviews.

But she need not have feared, because the following week after the interviews, which had been spread over a whole day, she was advised she had done well. She now had to apply to colleges and universities offering the course. It was late to apply, and early August before she had dates of attendance at the University of Sussex, and the London Polytechnic. She had chosen these because she felt she could travel to daily or weekly to either of them if she secured a place. Sussex only offered her a place on their reserve list, and their course would commence in April 1978. The London Poly wanted her to start in January 1978. At least she had a place, but when she contacted Social Services Head Office she was advised by the clerk dealing with the bursaries that if she were granted one she would have to start in September that year 1977, the money could not be held over. Everything was against her. She contacted the tutor on her present course and explained her dilemma. Firstly she had not yet been granted the bursary and if she was she had to start at a course within a few weeks.

'Well Maggie I think you will have to ring round other colleges. I hear that Ipswich College in Suffolk start their course in September, try there.' She advised.

'Thanks Jennie,' she put down the phone and dialled directory enquiries and established the telephone number for the college at Ipswich. She was put through to the Social Studies Department and spoke to a very friendly tutor. She explained her dilemma and asked if there was any chance of a placement with them.

'Well as luck would have it, I think we can help, but you will have to come for interview, and we would have to ensure you are suitable for placement,' he told her. He gave her a date for the following Monday.

She received a telephone call from the Social Services Department to say she had been awarded a bursary.

She could not believe her ears. She had a bursary, but it had to be used by the end of September. She had no choice, she could not take up placement in London, nor in Brighton, her only chance was Ipswich. Everything hung on it.

She told Gary she was going to Ipswich the following Monday. He just stared at her. 'You said you would get a placement near to home not in Suffolk, have you gone out of your mind?' he raved. She tried to explain it to him, but he was not interested. He went out of the front door, slamming it behind him. The glass rattled in the door, and Sadie jumped up out of her basket, wondering what was going on. She knew he was angry, but she did not care, she was determined now to do all she could to get a placement.

CHAPTER 26

Margaret was in a whirl. She had a possible place, and she had funding for Phase 3 of the course but Gary was saying she could not go. She telephoned Jennie her tutor at Southampton College and explained the situation.

'Maggie I do feel you should grasp this opportunity while it is available to you, it is not something that will be repeated, you would have to start all over again on the two year course,' she told her.

'Yes I know Jennie but my husband is adamant I cannot go, whatever can I do?' she wailed.

'I think you had better convince him to come down here to the college and I will talk to him,' Jennie replied.

'I do not think he will come, but I will try.' Margaret put down the telephone and dreaded trying to talk Gary into going to see Jennie.

That evening she cooked his favourite dinner, rack of Lamb with roast potatoes and vegetables. She knew he was not working that evening, which would give her the opportunity to talk to him.

He appeared in a good humour, especially after dinner, so she took the bull by the horns and asked him if he would go with her the following day to Southampton and talk to her tutor. He sat for quite some while before saying 'Okay I will go, but I will not agree to you going on this course in Suffolk, and that is final.'

A partial victory, she thought. Now it would be up to Jennie.

So the following day they set out in silence for Southampton, and arrived at the college at morning break time. She asked the receptionist to page Jennie and they all met in the refectory and had coffee. Gary shook hands with Jennie and she explained to him the need for the course to be taken now, and that funding was not available for the colleges nearer to home because of their starting dates. Gary seemed mesmerised by her tutor, who was a lovely lady, who appeared to cajole him into accepting it was in Margaret's best interest to go, and that she would only be gone Monday to Friday each week, and would be home for weekends and the long college breaks, and that the course would end in June the following year.

Margaret could not believe it when he agreed that she could go. She felt jubilant, but terrified he would change his mind, and put obstacles in the way, but he did not. He told Jennie the family could manage so long as Margaret came home every weekend. So the die was cast.

She went to Suffolk the following Monday for her interview. It was most unusual. There were other candidates there, and they were each given a topic to talk about for five minutes in front of everyone else. Her topic was a razor blade. She never realised five minutes could last so long, but she managed to talk at length about the uses of a razor blade, what it looked like, and who used them. She was interviewed by two of the course lecturers about her reasons for going on the course, and by 3pm she was on her way home.

Two weeks later the college confirmed she had been given a place. She was to start on the 19th September, just one week ahead. Margaret found she was rushing around shopping and cooking pies and puddings and placing them in the freezer. She changed all the beds, and did all washing and ironing, at the same time as packing a suitcase for herself. She had books to take and folders to buy. She was so busy she almost forgot she had nowhere to stay in Ipswich. The following day she went to see Sam Jackson, who suggested she telephone the local Education Welfare

Officer in Suffolk and ask for some help. This she did. A very nice lady called Joan Summers.

When she telephoned, Joan said there was little time to find somewhere, but suggested she went to stay with her for the first two weeks, and that she would look out for anyone offering lodgings. She had a spare room that Margaret could use until her son returned home. Margaret was delighted. This would give her time to find somewhere once she got to Ipswich.

She went to talk with her home help Joan Beak and asked for her help with the family whilst she was away. Joan was a brick, and agreed she would look after Katy, collect her from school each afternoon, and prepare the evening meal, as well as do the housework. Gary was happy that Joan was going to cover for her, he liked Joan because she fussed over him, and made him feel important.

So the following Sunday evening she set off for Ipswich and arrived about 9pm at Joan Summers' house. When she knocked on the front door of the very nice detached house in Princes Avenue, the front door flew open and a very jolly lady in her forties welcomed her.

'Come in my dear, leave the suitcase in the hall here and come and have a cup of tea, I am sure you could do with one after that long journey?' she ushered Margaret into the sitting room, where a girl of Katy's age was doing her homework at the table.

'Maggie meet Jodie my daughter, she is quite excited that we are having a guest stay for a short while,' she ushered Margaret toward the sofa. 'Sit down and I will pop the kettle on.' She turned and walked toward the kitchen.

Margaret looked around. It was a nice comfortable house, the lounge was beautifully decorated, with magnolia coloured walls and warm plum coloured curtains. The chairs were large and comfortable to sit in. She eased herself back into the cushions on the sofa and congratulated herself on how lucky she was to be there.

Jodie appeared to be quite shy. Margaret smiled at her and asked what sort of homework she was doing.

'It is an essay, I have to write about Africa, but I do not know a lot about it,' she explained.

'Africa is a vast country, with deserts and wild game parks. Then there is the beautiful waterfalls at Victoria, and right at the bottom is Table Mountain in South Africa. If I can be of any help, please ask,' she smiled at Jodie. 'On the other hand perhaps no one is supposed to help you?' she questioned.

Jodie explained she had seen a film on the video at school all about that country, and she had a couple of books from the school library to help her, but her problem was actually writing it down. As the essay did not have to be in until Wednesday, Margaret agreed to read it the following evening when she returned from college.

Joan returned with a tray and cups and saucers, and a plate of dainty sandwiches and cakes. 'I thought you might be hungry, so do help yourself Maggie while I pour the tea.' Margaret suddenly realised she had missed dinner. She had cooked dinner at home for the family but had been too busy with everything she had forgotten to have a meal herself; so she was grateful for the sandwiches, which were delicious.

Joan asked Margaret all about the course she was going on, and about the arrangements she had made for her family. It was suddenly half past ten. Jodie had taken herself upstairs to get ready for bed. Joan took the tray back into the kitchen, and then showed Margaret up to the room she was sleeping in. It was quite small but had a nice divan bed, covered by a beautiful blue quilt which matched the curtains. A small chest of drawers was against the opposite wall, and had a triple mirror on the top. There was no wardrobe but she noticed a curtain hanging in the corner, and was told there was a rail with a few hangers there if she needed to hang anything up.

It felt cosy, and the bathroom along the passage was exquisite. She longed to get into the marble bath, but confined herself to a quick wash and to clean her teeth, before going to bed.

The following morning, breakfast was a very rushed affair, with Jodie quickly eating a bowl of cereal, and putting on her blazer, and Joan busy answering the telephone while trying to eat a piece of toast and drink her tea. After eating a leisurely boiled egg with toast and a cup of tea, Margaret made her way to the college.

It was a huge building with seven floors. Trying to find a place in the college car park had been a feat of ingenuity. Her car was a large Datsun Laurel. Most of the cars were small. No doubt the students went for cheap to run cars, and ones easy to park. She made her way into the building. There were students flying this way and that. She headed for the lifts. She knew she was going to room 708 on the 7th floor.

As she entered the lift, a man older than herself stepped inside. She asked him which floor he wanted. He smiled and said he wanted floor 6. So she pressed the buttons for both the 6th and the 7th floors.

When the lift stopped at floor 6, the man stepped out and thanked her. She thought he must be one of the lecturers. He was smartly dressed in a brown suit and was carrying a briefcase. She carried on up to floor 7 and made her way to room 708. Inside there was a babble of voices, all sorts of people talking in small groups, and two men on the dais talking together.

She looked around and to her surprise saw Jenny from Hampshire talking to a man she knew to be another EWO from Hampshire. She walked over to them, and Jenny said, 'Why hello, so you managed to get on this course Maggie after all?' They hugged each other, and Margaret explained that hers had been a last minute thing but yes she had managed it.

'Oh great,' Jenny said, 'nice to have some of the old team on board. Maggie have you met Patrick? He was EWO for Denton, not far from your home town.'

Margaret smiled at Patrick. 'Yes I remember seeing you at staff meetings at Winchester,' she told him. While they were talking together the door of the room opened again. She turned to see who it was, and was surprised to see the man who had been in the lift with her. They looked at each other from across the room, then smiled at each other. They both knew he had got off at the wrong floor.

Margaret turned round and found their small group had been joined by a slim lady with curly hair. She learnt that her name was Brenda and she lived in Hampshire too. Brenda was a social worker in Dorset just across the border, and had been sponsored by that county.

The tutors on the dais called everyone to order, and asked them to take a seat. The desks were placed right round the outside of the room on three sides, forming a horseshoe shape. The smaller of the tutors smiled and said, 'May I introduce myself I am Michael Penn, and my colleague is John Miles. We will be your main course tutors during the next ten months. We will be joined by a Psychologist Philip Wayne, and a Sociologist Henry Potter. Hopefully we will help you all to attain the CQSW certificate by the time the course ends in June next year.'

'If there are any questions anyone would like to ask, do please raise them, and I will try to answer them.' He looked round the group. Everyone sat still, although there were lots of questions Margaret wanted to ask, but she did not want to appear forward, she knew she would soon find out the answers shortly.

'Perhaps I can start by saying that anyone who does not have accommodation go and see a lady in the office wing near the main entrance called Miss Hamilton, who keeps a list of lodgings in the area if you are interested.' Michael told them. 'Also everyone in the building calls me Mike, so do feel free to call me that.'

He went on to give them all timetables of lectures, and a layout of the college. He told them that their group of 19 members was unique, and the only course like it totally made up of senior staff from County Councils and Voluntary Agencies. The reason being, there were few staff who were qualified in social work departments and much of the work of the departments was at present being carried out by unqualified staff. It was up to colleges like theirs to ensure staff became qualified to fill qualified vacancies as soon as possible.

So the course started. They all quickly found the refectory, and small groups met there regularly, when there were no lectures or after lessons. Margaret found the college had a fantastic library, and also had sports facilities on campus. It made her feel young again, and she soon put aside her worries about what was happening at home. She would soon find out when she went home at the weekend.

She formed a strong allegiance with Jenny, Patrick and Brenda, and the four of them agreed that it would be sensible if they all shared the travelling at weekends back to Hampshire, taking it in turns to drive all four of them. They devised a plan that they would drive to Margaret's house and that Jenny's husband Terry or Brenda's boyfriend Tim would meet there and drive the two ladies the rest of the way to the south of the county. They decided to drop off Patrick first, and on the return journey pick him up last. So the pact was formed. This would save her a lot of money in petrol, so Margaret was very happy with the arrangement.

CHAPTER 27

The first week at college gave her an insight into the content of the course and what subjects they would be studying. Lectures were scattered over the week and she soon learnt that she had a lot to learn. She attended lectures on Human growth and development; the Acts of Parliament and how they are implemented with regard to court procedures. These involved all the children's acts, the divorce laws and the law pertaining in mental health, in fact everything that came under the umbrella of social work.

Essays would be set, and these would be discussed with your tutorial tutor. Margaret had Michael Penn as her tutor and she knew she would be seeing him once a fortnight for an hour to discuss her progress.

She really felt it was a mammoth task in front of her, but having come so far she was not prepared to give up. Firstly she must find some lodgings she could only stay with Joan Summers for a maximum of two weeks, when her son returned from abroad.

One of the students she had recently met called Dorothy heard that she was looking for lodgings and told her there was room where she was staying. So Margaret went with Dorothy in the lunch break to an address just two roads from the college. Margaret was amazed, it had broken windows and holes in the floor of the kitchen. A woman in tatty clothes showed her round, and explained that to get to the room which was available she would have to cross someone else's room. She learnt this was a man's room. *I can't possibly live here,* she thought. The whole place was dilapidated and run down. The kitchen was filthy. She thanked the woman for showing her round, and then turned and thanked Dorothy for considering her, but said she had somewhere else to look at first. She made up her mind she would go and see the lady Michael Penn had mentioned at the college, and see if she could find something better.

She went to see the lady in the reception area, Miss Hamilton, the following day. When Margaret knocked on her door, she heard a welcoming 'come in' from within. She was a kindly lady in her fifties, who obviously enjoyed mothering people. 'Come in my dear,' she smiled at Margaret, 'now how can I help you?' she asked.

'Well I have just started the social work course and I need to find lodgings in the area as soon as possible,' she told her. 'I went to see somewhere yesterday, but I could not possibly live there, it was awful.'

'Oh I see, well I believe I can help you, what are you actually looking for, a room, or full board?' she started to look through a file on her desk.

'I am not sure, I think I would like a room. Somewhere I can cook breakfast and have my meals during the rest of the day, here at the college,' she explained.

'Well I might have just the thing, Miss Jarvis is looking for a tenant. She lives quite near the college and has a three bedroomed house. She is the daughter of a vicar, who unfortunately passed away a few years ago. She has limited funds and benefits from taking in some of our students. However she does prefer mature students, and I think you fall in that category. She also likes ladies.' Miss Hamilton smiled at Margaret. 'She is offering a large room which has a sink and a small cooker, and a gas fire. There is a bathroom and you can have a bath once a week. She provides all bed linen, but she does not like a lot of noise or students inviting guests into the room. She currently has a young man in another room, but I believe he is leaving shortly to share a house with other students. The rent is £5 a week,' she looked up, 'how does that sound to you?'

'It sounds just what I am looking for,' Margaret smiled back.

'Well I will give you her address and you can pop along to see her, she is at home a lot of the time. She is on the telephone, but I am sure she will not mind you just calling.' She wrote down the address. Margaret thanked her and made her way out of the college.

At the end of the day she drove out of the college car park and headed in the direction of Joan Summers' house. Joan had prepared dinner. She sat at the table next to Jodie and discussed her day at school. Jodie told her that she hoped to complete her essay about Africa that evening and would love Margaret to read it, and give her opinion. They made plans for Margaret to read it the following evening, just as Joan came in with the plated meals. It was delicious, roast chicken with all the trimmings.

Over dinner she told Joan about her visit to Miss Hamilton, and the possibility of lodgings in Sycamore Avenue.

'Well that is great. It is a nice area, I will draw you the directions so you can call on the good lady. Let us keep our fingers crossed, it suits you.' Joan said.

So the following day after her last lecture she drove to number 13 Sycamore Avenue. She hoped number thirteen was not unlucky in any way. She parked on the grass verge outside the driveway and walked up to the front door and rang the bell. A dog barked, or rather yapped.

She heard a door close inside the house before the front door opened and a little old lady smiled at her. Margaret thought she was nearer seventy than fifty.

'Hello Miss Jarvis?' she asked. 'I am Maggie Pearce, I have been given your name and address by the college. I believe you have a room to let?'

Miss Jarvis invited Margaret in. She could hear the yapping coming from along the corridor. 'I hope you do not mind dogs. I have a small poodle who keeps me company, she makes a fuss when people come, but she is a nice dog though. Come into my sitting room.' Margaret followed her into a small sitting room with a table and two chairs, and two fireside chairs and a sideboard on which were books and photographs. 'Do sit down my dear,' she ushered Margaret into the other fireside chair.

Margaret explained that she needed a room five days a week, Monday to Friday, that she would be travelling home every weekend to Hampshire. She was happy with the rent and would pay in advance each week.

Miss Jarvis explained about her other tenant, a young man, and that he would be leaving in two weeks, and asked her if she knew of anyone else needing accommodation. Margaret said she did not know of anyone at present, but would keep her ears open as she felt sure there were other students who might be looking for a room. Miss Jarvis explained she would prefer someone older than her current tenant, who she implied played his radio loud and came home late at night. 'I think older people are more responsible, don't you?' she asked. Margaret smiled and nodded.

So it was arranged she would move in the following Sunday evening, after her first weekend at home. She would bring her teasmade with her.

She returned to Joan Summers' house, and after another superb meal, she sat down with Jodie and read her essay. It was very good, the child had put a lot of thought into writing it, but had left out one or two things Margaret felt she should include. So having talked about it, the essay was improved.

Joan Summers said, 'I think she should get top marks now.'

The rest of the first week sped by.

******

On Friday afternoon after classes the group of four set off for Hampshire. It had been decided that Margaret would drive that weekend. She was pleased about this because she knew she would need her car at home over the weekend. On other weekends she would have to make some other arrangements about transport.

They agreed the route they would take, and stopped halfway near Hatfield at a café for tea and a toasted teacake. Jenny then rang her husband and told them what time roughly they would be in Harmsworth. He would collect her and Brenda from Margaret's house.

So they circled London to the north and made their way to Denton to drop Patrick off, then on to Harmsworth. When they arrived, tired but glad to have completed the journey, Margaret made them all a cup of tea before Terry arrived to take the ladies to the south of the county.

Katy was excited that her mother was home, and Sarah wanted to bring her up to date with what had been happening in her absence. Gary looked pleased to see her, and helped her cook the evening meal.

She explained she had enjoyed staying with Joan Summers and her daughter, and that she had found some lodgings with an elderly lady on the other side of town.

Over the weekend Gary made love to her and was very attentive, and said they had managed quite well in her absence with the help of Joan Beak. He did not think it would be a problem. Margaret felt elated; perhaps things were improving. On the Saturday she went shopping and stocked up the cupboards. She did piles of washing, and as it was a nice day, managed to get everything dry ready for ironing.

Sunday morning she did the ironing and put everything ready for the following week, then set to, to make a few ready meals. She made up a casserole and placed it in the freezer as well as a cheesecake. She made a cottage pie, and ensured there were sausages and bacon in the fridge. There were plenty of vegetables and fruit, she was sure they would be all right for the next week.

She loaded her teasmade into the car boot as well as her old typewriter, which she would need to write her essays with. It was a good job her boot was very large, it had to accommodate four people's luggage.

At 4pm Terry arrived with Jenny and Brenda, and they set off to collect Patrick before returning to Ipswich. They were all cheerful and talked about their weekends. Margaret mentioned she had taken two books home from the college library, but had not had time to read either of them. She promised herself that she would do so during the evenings after lessons.

Brenda had been ballroom dancing over the weekend with her boyfriend Tim. They had been having lessons for quite a while and entered competitions regularly.

Jenny had spent a very pleasant weekend with her husband. Her son was training to be a policeman and her daughter lived in Surrey with her husband and children. They had been on their own this weekend and had been busy gardening.

Patrick explained that his wife had not been happy he had no car for the weekend, but it was decided he would drive everyone home the following weekend, then he would have his car to take his wife out.

So all in all everything seemed to be working. Week two was in front of them.

Margaret moved into 13 Sycamore Avenue. She soon became friendly with the little dog, whose name was Fifi. She loved attention and being stroked. From that day on she could often be found up in Margaret's room, sitting on the rug Margaret had brought with her. She had made it herself. Her brother John had taught her how to buy the canvas and wool, and knot the loops and follow a pattern painted on the canvas.

Miss Jarvis did not seem to mind Fifi being up with Margaret, but said if she was a nuisance to send her downstairs. Miss Jarvis liked Margaret, and over the coming months they often had a cup of tea together and a chat. She was very interested in the course that was being studied.

During Margaret's second week Miss Jarvis reminded her to look out for someone to fill the other room, and that she would be most grateful. During lunch in the refectory on Tuesday Jenny told her that Mark Reynolds was not happy with his lodgings and was looking for somewhere a little better.

'Well there is a vacancy at the house I am staying,' she told Jenny. 'I'll have a word with Mark, which one is he?' she enquired.

'The one who sits in the far right hand corner near the window,' Jenny replied.

How ironic she thought, he was the man she had met in the lift.

Later that afternoon she approached him and told him about the room which was vacant. 'Well that would be great, I'll call round and see the good lady this evening.'

She later learnt that he had arranged to move in the following week after the young man departed. Miss Jarvis mentioned it the following morning just as Margaret was leaving for the college. 'I believe I must thank you for introducing me to Mark. I must admit I had hoped for another woman, but he seems pleasant enough.' She opened the door for Margaret, who bent down and stroked Fifi, and saying goodbye.

The third week Margaret learnt the title of her first essay. A Project she had to study before writing about it. 'The class structure.' This meant a couple of evenings staying late in the library. So she saw little of Mark Reynolds. The following weekend it was agreed they would return home for the weekend in Brenda's 1100 car. It was going to be a squeeze it was quite tiny. Brenda said that Tim wanted to check it over for her so she needed to take it back to Hampshire. It was agreed, however they had hardly left Ipswich when the fan broke. Jenny gave up her stockings to make a temporary repair, but Patrick said there was no way they could drive to Hampshire like that, so they drove back into Ipswich and took Jenny's car which Brenda drove.

The cost of meals in the refectory were subsidised but even so money was tight. Brenda and Margaret decided to share the cost. Brenda bought a small brown loaf, and Margaret provided lettuce and tomatoes to go with the mushroom omelettes the cook kindly made them each evening. It was quite a monotonous diet but they both enjoyed it.

On her fourth weekend home she learnt from Peter that he was planning on getting married the following year to Kathy. Margaret suggested they were still quite young, and it was quite an expensive thing to do but he was quite positive about it. She knew he still owed money on his motorbike.

Sarah was enjoying her course at the local college, but spent some time at Margaret's sister's house. Gary had taken on calling on May and her husband, whilst Margaret was in Suffolk. Margaret knew that her brother-in-law was quite ill and been attending the hospital, and that it was likely he would undergo an operation shortly to remove one of his lungs. He was a chain smoker and it was feared he had cancer.

The first half term just flew by. She had taken to play Squash with the others one evening a week, and occasionally their small group would go swimming at the local baths. She also took to taking a walk some evenings. On one particular evening she was just leaving the house in Sycamore Avenue when Mark appeared, and said he was thinking of taking a walk as well. He asked if he could walk with her. She nodded. They walked toward town just strolling along. They started to talk a bit about themselves, and as they were about to pass an old secondhand shop they stopped and mused over the contents of the window. There were old medals in the middle and Mark told her he had some medals from when he had served in the RAF during the war. He had been awarded a DFM along with several other medals. They started to talk about the war, and she told him all she knew about it was when she had been evacuated to North Wales between 1942 and 1945, although she had remembered the doodlebugs coming over and shrapnel being dropped, and the sirens sounding, with people rushing down into dugouts. She found him most interesting to talk to, and they spent quite a few evenings just walking, often ending up in the local pub for a drink before returning to their lodgings.

He told her about his job in Yorkshire, he worked in Social Services as an unqualified social worker. Many of his clients were elderly or had a mental health problem. She told him about her job in Education and how she so much wanted to be qualified as a social worker. That she loved working with children the most.

Mark had a wonderful sense of humour, and a very kind personality. She felt comfortable with him. Margaret was not sure that Miss Jarvis was happy about their friendship, she often implied things in passing to Margaret.

Margaret also knew Miss Jarvis wanted her to sit with her some evenings, and saw Mark as a rival. However, Margaret took little notice, it was nice to enjoy herself, and do her own thing.

It was agreed she would drive all the group home at half term, as Brenda's car was still broken down, Jenny did not need her car as Terry had his, and Patrick had arranged to borrow one for the two weeks they had at home.

CHAPTER 28

It was nice to be at home with the girls, although the weather was rather inclement they enjoyed a couple of trips out and visiting family members during the week the girls had off school. Margaret would have a two week break before going back to Ipswich, so there would be lots of time to organise her time away for the next six weeks.

One thing she knew she would do was to visit her brother-in-law in hospital. May had told her on the telephone that Fred had endured a horrible operation where they had removed one of his lungs. He was now getting out of bed and had the physiotherapists walking him slowly, short distances, and encouraging him to breathe with his one lung, which he found difficult and tiring.

She drove to the hospital and found he was in a side ward in ICU. He was his usual cheerful self, though you could tell he was under a lot of strain. Margaret went and kissed him and talked with him for a short while before May arrived.

When she left to go shopping, she felt very tearful. He was such a nice man, it was awful to see him so poorly, and the prognosis was not good. She had taken the time to talk to the senior nurse on duty, who told her that he was not responding well at present, but hoped he would improve in the next week.

Margaret drove into town firstly to see Sam Jackson, but found he was away on holiday. She continued to the supermarket and bought the necessary provisions for the following week. Many things came in tins which were easy to open. Baked beans, soups, tinned meats, tinned fruit, but at least there was lots in the stock cupboard, besides her baking in the freezer and ready meals she had cooked.

She bade the family farewell the following Sunday evening and returned to Ipswich. She knew the following day the whole group was going to stay for three days at the Bay Hotel in Felixstowe. Michael Penn had told her in her last tutorial that the tutors felt the group were not gelling well enough, so that it had been decided to take a couple of days out from study and get to know each other better.

When she arrived at The Bay Hotel she soon learned that everyone was in one of the meeting rooms and they were firstly going to play a game of Crocodiles. She had never heard of it, and was anxious about it. She soon found that it was quite fun. The object was to ensure you did not fall in the water, and had to jump from area to area, because if you did it was assumed you would be eaten by a crocodile. The gaps between the area became larger, and only being small she found it hard to take large leaps, and on her fourth jump she landed in the so called water. But she found that her colleagues pulled her out, and she was safe.

They then played a game of Stars. This was a thinking game and everyone found this game much more difficult. Apparently the object was to ensure the other people did not win, and you had to use your initiative to survive. Margaret did not fare well on this game, she found she was trying to help some of the others make achievements.

The food in the hotel was good, and meals lasted a long time, with people in the group talking non stop. The tutors ensured everyone changed places every so often, so you had different people to talk with. Envelopes were handed round with suggestions of what to talk about. They had a plenary session at the end of the afternoon on the second day and discussion of what to do on the third day. It was decided that each person, now they felt more comfortable with their colleagues, would be able to stand up and talk for a short while on their background and why they were on the course.

At the last dinner on the third evening wine was provided, and afterwards they broke up into small groups and walked along Felixstowe beach. The stars were out, and it was not cold. Margaret enjoyed it. She walked with Jenny and Brenda, and just behind them was Dorothy, Sean and Mark. About 9pm they all dispersed to return to their lodgings in Ipswich. It had been a remarkable three days.

On the Thursday they were put into three groups. They were told that each group would study a particular theme. Group one would study Depression, Group two would study The Juvenile Court, and Group three would study Hospitals - and the Elderly.

Margaret was placed in group one along with Luke, Leonard, Rose and Nora; none of the group that she knew well, but had talked with at the hotel. Now she knew why they had to get to know each other better. It was decided at their first meeting that Margaret would visit a Psychiatric Hospital and interview a Psychiatrist and find out as much information as possible on depression and report back. Sean who already worked in a mental health hospital would find out information about patients and how they were treated. Leonard who was 'all mouth and no trousers' conveniently opted to be the speaker when they came to give feedback. Rose and Nora agreed to act the parts of patients when they came to give a performance about their subject at the end of the following term. They had three months to prepare things.

That evening when she went for a walk with Mark she told him about their project and that she felt she had the worst deal getting all the facts and information. Mark told her his group were enacting a Juvenile Court Scene and he was to be the solicitor for the defence. He soon started to be called Perry Mason, by his group members.

Her first essay had to be handed in by the end of the autumn term, and she was hard pressed to put together all the information on the Class Structure and type an essay about it. She spent most of her evenings typing in her room with Fifi laying on her rug, and helping her eat her sandwiches.

Mark told her he was taking his essay back to his office in Yorkshire, and asking them to type it for him. They continued to meet up at the college, playing squash with some of the others and taking evening walks when time allowed.

Just before the end of term Rose suggested that everyone meet together for a party at the lodgings she shared with Natasha at the local hospital. Some people took food, and some brought wine, and Margaret agreed to supply music. The weekend before the party she asked her son Peter to make up some tapes of party music without telling his dad. She took a long black dress with her to college, which had a skirt of rainbow colours. The party went well, and Margaret ending up dancing with Mark. As they were both going to the same venue she went in his car. At the end of the evening they drove back to the lodgings together and said goodnight. It had been fun.

So she prepared to return home for Christmas. She knew she would have lots to do, but was aware she had more studying to do as tutors had given out the title of the second essay.

'The Study of Sociology is of Significance in the Education and Training of Social Workers'. Discuss.

They were studying Sociology with Henry Potter, but the whole group found him rather pompous, and someone who had little time for social workers. She decided that she would take home a couple of books on Sociology from the college library and make sure she found time to read them. She must also make an appointment to see the Psychiatrist at Fenton Park Mental Hospital. She knew his name was Dr Linton, and soon after her return home she rang the hospital and spoke to his secretary and asked to have an appointment to see him during the first week of January.

She learnt that May's husband was at home but still very ill. He was being taken to the hospital regularly, but his breathing was poor and he was getting weaker.

Margaret had her work cut out to prepare for Christmas. She learnt that her mother was going to her brother John's for Christmas, so there would be just her own family.

Peter was bringing Kathy, and Sarah was bringing her boyfriend Jack. He was a nice lad and often came and collected Sarah for a trip to the cinema or meeting up with friends. She made a Christmas cake and a Christmas pudding, and ordered a small turkey from the butcher. Katy helped her put up the decorations and she acquired a small Christmas tree, and put some tinsel and coloured balls on in. Gary seemed to keep out of the way; he told her that the taxi firm he worked for was terribly busy at present and he was doing more hours. When he was home he kept coming up behind her and putting his arms around her. She resented this, for some reason she did not want him anywhere near her. She tried to make a joke of it at times, but often she became irritable and asked him to go away. His reaction on one occasion was to hit her, but she just walked away. She succumbed to his lovemaking twice over the Christmas holiday, but she knew she was just letting him use her, she laid impassive, staring at the ceiling, he did not seem to notice; she had no feelings for him whatsoever.

During the week after Christmas she received a phone call from Dr Linton's secretary to say he had a free afternoon the following Tuesday and Margaret could go for two o'clock. She thanked the woman and organised a file and wrote down some questions she needed to ask the Psychiatrist.

It was a huge hospital. She had visited various small buildings in the grounds when she had been working. One was used for patients who suffered from alcoholism, and another by elderly patients who were geriatric, and could not be cared for in the community.

She made her way to the main building and found the door marked Dr Linton and knocked. Dr Linton opened the door to her and took her into his office. She explained the project she was studying and asked him a wealth of questions. He was a very quiet man and did not interrupt her often. After an hour his secretary brought in a tray of tea and biscuits, which was some relief. Afterwards he took her on a ward round explaining the difference between one type of depression and another. She found it fascinating. All too soon it was time to leave, but she knew she had lots of information to take back to her colleagues.

On her return to college the following week she had a tutorial with Michael Penn, when he told her, her first essay had passed, and he had been most impressed with her arguments. *So far so good* she thought. However she was not looking forward to writing the second essay. She had taken time to read as much as she could about Sociology during her Christmas break, but she found it complicated. She would go to the library and change the books, and work out a strategy.

Mark was well under way with his essay, but told her one evening that the lady who usually typed for him at his offices in Yorkshire was not available to type his second essay. Margaret offered to type it for him.

'Would you really?' he said, 'that would be great if you would.' So as well as reading for her own essay, she was typing his. He came into her room and sat with her when there were passages she did not understand. Apparently his subjects were different to hers. She liked his nearness, and it felt so right to be there together . . . So peaceful.

She struggled with her writing, but eventually within a week she had completed not only Mark's essay but also her own, and they were handed in.

She received a phone call from her mother to say that Fred had died, and the funeral was being held the following Friday. Margaret told her tutor Michael and arranged to leave for home on Wednesday. She sought out her fellow travellers and explained the situation so that they could make arrangements without her for the following weekend. She packed her things and explained to Miss Jarvis, who commiserated with her, and set off for home. It seemed strange to be driving by herself, she was so used to the group journeys now.

Everyone at home was sad. Sarah who had become quite close to Fred and was terribly upset. Katy hardly knew him, and could not understand what was going on.

Margaret looked out her black suit and a black skirt for Sarah. She arranged for Joan Beak to look after Katy for the afternoon of the funeral. Her sister, quite naturally was inconsolable, and it was some relief when the funeral at the crematorium was over. Margaret went back to her sister's house for a sandwich and a cup of tea, but her sister kept jibing her about being away from home saying, 'Your place is at home with your family.' Margaret left soon after, she could not expect May to understand, she did not have her mortgage to pay or all those bills.

As she had driven home by herself she had to drive back the following Sunday evening on her own as well. But she felt glad to be going back.

Mark was already at Sycamore Avenue when she returned. He appeared pleased to see her, and suggested a walk. It was very cold being January, but she readily agreed. He tucked his arm through hers, and said, 'Margaret I would like to thank you for typing my essay, how would you like to go out for a meal one evening?' She did not know what to say, but smiled and said she wouldn't mind it sounded a nice idea. So they made a date for Wednesday evening.

They told Miss Jarvis that they were going out for a meal, she did not look overly pleased but wished them a good evening. Margaret realised she had not sat with Miss Jarvis recently. She had been so busy with one thing or another, what with the essays and having to go home for the funeral, and any spare evenings she was swotting or staying late at the library. Any spare time she would go for a short walk with Mark.

He took her to a hotel in Needham Market a village not far from Ipswich. She wore her long black dress with the coloured lines on the skirt. The bodice and sleeves were made of wool and she needed the warmth as it was very cold.

They had a very nice meal, but she was cross with him for letting her order a dessert and then abstaining himself. He watched her try to wade through a plate of sherry trifle. He kept laughing at her trying to eat it all. When they left the hotel they decided to drive to Felixstowe and walk along the beach. Although cold, it was very pleasant, and they walked arm in arm. She felt so relaxed with him. As they turned to retrace their footsteps, he turned her to face him and pulled her towards him and kissed her. The world stopped. He immediately apologised, but she told him it was all right she had not minded. Minded - it had been heaven. What a beautiful end to a beautiful evening.

CHAPTER 29

At the beginning of February the group were given the titles of the third and final essay. Margaret looked at her title in amazement. She had no idea of where to begin, or even to understand the question.

'It is your job (when the chips are down) to accept Society's expressed view of the kind and amount of mutual aid that it can afford, and then reconcile the victims and losers as best as you can to their lot'. Discuss.

That evening she talked it over with Mark at the local pub, and after some discussion she felt she understood what was expected as an answer, all she had to do was argue the case, for and against. She was so grateful for his laid back attitude. His own question did not appear easy, it was about Widows. These essays had to be handed in by the end of March, just prior to the Easter holidays.

The tutors advised the group that beside their normal lectures and studying, they were each going to be placed with an outside agency for two weeks prior to Easter. This caused some stirrings, and everyone was talking about this for days.

At the end of that week, Mark learnt he was being placed at the Probation Department at Bury St Edmunds, Ashley was going to work in the soup kitchens in London, and Jenny was being placed at the Turner Village for handicapped children. Margaret learnt she would be going to the Social Services Department at Basildon in Essex and would be staying at one of the Old People's homes in their guest suite.

She looked forward to her placement, but knew she would miss Mark's company. On the 26th February she made her way to Basildon on her own. Each of the group would need their own cars. She found the retirement home which was run by the local council, and the warden showed her to the guest suite, where she unpacked. There was a very comfortable bedroom with en suite bathroom, and a small kitchen next door which all the staff used to make tea and coffee, or warm something up to eat.

Around 9 o'clock before going to bed she wandered around the home and came across a little old lady who asked Margaret if she could take her home, she did not like it there. Margaret reassured her that it was very nice and that she was staying herself, and walked with the lady down to the staff room. She found a member of staff, who admonished the little old lady about leaving her room, and hurried her along the corridor. Most of the residents were in bed, many of them snoring.

She went into the big kitchen and acquired a small amount of milk, which she took upstairs to the tiny kitchen and made a cup of tea before going to bed.

The following morning she had some breakfast before driving to the Social Services Department in the centre of the town. The offices were very much like the offices in Harmsworth, laid out communally. She was introduced to Angela who was to be her supervisor for two weeks; a young girl no more than 24 years of age. Angela sat and talked with her for some while, and said she was in awe of supervising someone with as much knowledge and experience as Margaret. However Angela was the qualified one, and had gone straight from college to university to gain her qualification. She had no experience of married life, or of having children, and it became obvious that she relied on Margaret's sensible approach to situations which they came across.

To break the ice Angela invited Margaret to her flat for an evening meal on her second day. Angela had cooked Moussaka, but when it was placed in front of her, Margaret tried not to look aghast. There were lumps of minced meat and lumps of potato floating in a sea of fat on the plate. Margaret thought *I cannot possibly eat this* then remembered that this girl was going to write her appraisal. Gingerly she spiked a piece of meat and swallowed it, it was tasteless and oily. She spiked a piece of potato and ate it. How she got through the meal she did not know, but she ate anything that looked reasonably solid. She then thanked Angela for the meal, and made a hasty retreat. She felt sick.

She was given three cases to deal with. The first was a girl of 14 years of age called Alice whose parents were unable to control her. Margaret went to visit the family one evening and met the mother and stepfather, as well as Alice. The girl was very withdrawn and the parents volatile. She talked with the parents for some while on their own and then went up to Alice's bedroom and talked with her. She set the girl a task of drawing how she saw the family in relation to a house she had drawn roughly on a piece of paper, and said she would call and see Alice on her own the following Monday evening.

She was given a case of a family, where the father was stating his wife was an alcoholic and his daughters were at risk. Margaret visited the woman and soon learnt that she had lots of vodka bottles hidden all over the house and many empty bottles in the dustbin. The woman, Mrs Carey, told her that her husband was a lorry driver and away a lot, and she thought he was having affairs. Margaret confirmed with her that she only suspected this, and assured herself that the two daughters of the couple were not likely to come to any harm. She telephoned the husband and asked him to call and see her in the area office that Friday morning. She suggested to him that he join the local al-non group and also arrange an appointment for some counselling with the Marriage

Guidance Council. He said he was desperate, and agreed for her to make an appointment for them.

Her third client was a lady called Mrs Grice who was in her sixties and not long out of hospital having had a hysterectomy operation. Her children thought she was acting very strangely and feared she was going mad.

Margaret visited her and established a rapport with the woman. She told Margaret that whilst she was convalescing she was experiencing a bloated feeling in her abdomen and thought gremlins were invading her. Margaret suggested to the woman that when a hysterectomy is performed, the consultant often pumped in a lot of air into the abdomen cavity to be able to explore the area, and that there was possibly a lot of air still left in her abdomen. Mrs Grice looked at Margaret amazed but also listened to all she said. The following week when she returned to visit the woman she appeared quite normal and happy that her children now thought her capable of looking after their children and babysit for them.

When on duty she had been asked to attend a mental health section with her supervisor. Two children had locked themselves into the downstairs loo of a house on a council estate, and it was believed were hiding from their mother, who was known to the department as having a mental problem and was out of control. Margaret was told by her supervisor to talk to the woman through the front door letterbox, whilst the police went round the back of the house and gained access. It was not long before the services were in the house, and the good lady was taken into an ambulance and sectioned for 72 hours whilst Margaret talked to the children through the door of the downstairs loo, and told them that it was safe to come out. She then explained she would take them to a place of safety until their mother was well enough to look after them again. She took them to a local children's home, and stayed and had supper with them before returning to the lodgings at the old people's home.

The following week she returned to see Alice, who had filled in the people living in the family home on the drawing Margaret had given her. She had placed her mother in the main bedroom, and herself in the living room, but her stepfather she had placed outside the house in the far corner. Margaret realised the child was not coping, and did not see her stepfather as part of her family. She arranged an appointment for Alice at the Child Guidance Clinic, for two weeks time, and closed the case.

She was pleased to learn from her supervisor that she had been given an excellent appraisal. Margaret invited Angela to her lodgings and cooked her a meal of chicken in white wine sauce. Angela looked very sheepish, she praised Margaret for the dinner and apologised for the meal she had given Margaret the week before, saying she was no cook. There were still two portions of the chicken left, so on leaving the placement, she took the casserole with her and returned to Ipswich. She felt sure Mark would appreciate a chicken dinner.

When she arrived at Sycamore Avenue, she raced upstairs and placed the chicken casserole in her cooker. When she turned round she found a short note on her bed and a little silver genie lamp.

The note read, 'Dear Maggie, I am gutted, I have to remain at Bury St Edmunds for two more days to complete a report. Miss you, yours always, Mark.'

Margaret sat on her bed and the tears flowed down her cheeks. She suddenly realised that Mark meant so much to her, and he would not be there that week. In fact she suddenly realised that she loved him. He was so kind and thoughtful.

She had no appetite to eat, and when Fifi came upstairs to see her she gave the dog the chicken casserole. At least someone appreciated it. So she packed her things up ready for the journey home. She was feeling quite ill and upset and left for home on her own, two days before college broke up.

It was her brother and sister-in-law's silver wedding anniversary the following weekend and she promised to go to the small party which had been arranged. Gary was reasonably happy to go and it was a fairly pleasant occasion.

She had not been looking forward to the two weeks at home, but it gave her lots of time to study as well as talk with the girls. Peter and Kathy came and Kathy asked her if she would be kind enough to make her wedding dress and those of the bridesmaids. They had set their wedding for the first week in September.

Peter told her that unless she had any objection he would move into Kathy's house for the time being. With her away things between him and his father were not too good. Margaret said she had no objection. So that week Peter moved his things to Kathy's house. It would seem that after the wedding they had planned to live with Kathy's parents for a short while, and had put their name down on the council waiting list. This gave Margaret an idea.

When Gary came home one evening she told him that she did not want to live with him anymore. She pointed out that she had no feelings for him, and suggested that he move into the bedroom that Peter had just vacated. He looked at her aghast, but she was quite adamant about it, he knew she meant it, and the following weekend he moved into the third bedroom, which had just been vacated by Peter. She felt much better not to be sharing a bed with Gary.

When she returned to college after the Easter break she learnt that the college had arranged some day trips for them to Aldburgh, Felixstowe and Woodbridge as well as a full day's trip to Clacton-on-Sea, to visit a very unusual old people's home on the front.

Margaret sat with Mark on the coach, and they followed the group looking at all the different features of each area. The residential home at Clacton-on-Sea was fascinating. It was run by the residents, and they had their own bar and barman. The residents decided that they would have for meals and the staff were governed by the residents. It seemed to work reasonably well and everyone seemed happy.

Mark and Margaret walked along the front of Clacton enjoying the lovely sunshine and hand in hand. It was late April and everyone was enjoying the late spring weather. They walked into the town and were met by Dorothy and Sean. Dorothy took Mark aside and Margaret heard her say to him, 'There is no fool like an old fool' nodding towards her.

Dorothy knew they were both married and there could be many problems ahead, but she was implying that Margaret was using Mark whilst she was on the course, and just having a fling with him.

At the end of that week they all booked to have a meal in the hotel training section at the college. The college put on three course meals which were noted to be excellent. Their reputation was good and all the members of the group enjoyed the experience.

The third essays were handed in. One of the group, Leonard, appeared to sustain a heart attack, and was taken to hospital, so Brenda and Margaret typed his essay for him and handed it in.

Everyone was organised to go on a second placement. Mark was to be placed at St John's Mental Hospital at Lincoln, whereas Margaret was placed at St John's Hospital at Chelmsford. The two hospitals were miles apart. They would be in placement for a month. Brenda went to Probation at Braintree as well as Patrick. Jenny wanted to return to the Turner Village at Chelmsford. Margaret told her she would like to visit there for a day, and Jenny said she would arrange this if she could.

So after a turbulent weekend at home, Margaret drove to Chelmsford. She knew it was arranged she would be staying in the nurses' quarters for four weeks. She found her room was very small but adequate, and there was a kitchen a little further along the corridor to cook something if she needed to. However she soon found that the subsidised food in the staff canteen was terrific and usually dined there.

She missed Mark terribly, and was surprised to receive a telephone call from him to say he was coming down to Chelmsford to visit her during her first week. Her spirits rose. He arrived one afternoon and brought her a bunch of pink tulips. They walked around the grounds of the hospital and under the lovely magnolia trees. She felt so happy, but knew the visit was only a few short hours. Before he left he said to her, 'Maggie I know you have commitments at home, and so do I, but you are aware of my circumstances. I have no life at all at home and long to leave, but your situation is different.' He went on, 'if we were free I would love to pursue a relationship with you, I love you.'

She looked up at him and said, 'Mark I love you too, and yes I have commitments but my relationship with my husband is coming to a close.' She explained how things had changed over the last few months. 'I want to leave

Gary, I do not love him anymore and have not done so for some while.'

He pulled her into his arms and kissed her. 'We are going to be on placement for a month. I could not bear to not see you in that time. How do you feel about us meeting up somewhere between here and Lincoln each week?' he asked.

Her heart sang, 'I would love it,' she replied. So they arranged to meet the following week at St Neots, a small town in Cambridgeshire. They looked it up on the map and found it was accessible to the A1 for both of them.

During the following week she busied herself with ward visits and talking with consultants about situations concerning some of the patients. The first patient she was given was a girl of eight years old called Emily who was not eating. Her parents were concerned about her, and she had been admitted to the hospital for tests and observation.

Margaret arranged to visit Emily's family home in a village just north of the hospital called Witham. She met her mother and was introduced to her stepfather, both appeared very concerned about Emily. She then went to see Emily's teacher at the local school. Miss Phillips put a completely different complexion on things. She told Margaret that Emily ate well at school. She often had second helpings of dinner and spent money in the tuckshop on crisps and sweets. So Emily was eating at school but not at home. She realised the child wanted to worry her mother, and it was her way of trying to cope with her new stepfather who she resented. She relayed her findings to the consultant, who smiled and thanked her for her thorough investigation. Within a day Emily was discharged having been seen by a psychologist, who would continue to work with the family.

She made an appointment at the Family Planning Clinic in Chelmsford, she knew it would not be long before her and Mark made love. She was forty one years old. She could not afford to get pregnant, and did not feel it would be appropriate. She was put on the pill.

On the following weekend at home she measured up Kathy and the bridesmaids and went to Reading to purchase the material for the wedding outfits. She would have to find time over the next three or four months to complete the dresses. She had her work cut out, although she knew that the course would end at the end of June and she would have more time when back at home.

She did not like to think about the end of the course, she was just living one day at a time. Her life was in a muddle, and she could not see how to resolve it. Mark lived nearly three hundred miles up north, how were they ever going to see each other, or would things just come to an end? She could not bear contemplating the outcome. She did not want to stay with Gary, but she was married to him. Mark was married too, although from what he had told her he led a completely separate life from his wife and spent a lot of his time with his eldest son Jim when he was not working.

Why was life so horrible. She had prayed at Church for someone like Mark, and now everything was so complicated.

CHAPTER 30

On Wednesday 3rd May 1978 Margaret drove to St Neot's. She drove through the countryside from Chelmsford, passing through quaint little villages. The car radio was on and they were playing the latest Paul Young song 'Love is in the air'. She felt so happy, she was off to meet Mark.

She pulled into the small market town and found the car park; situated by the Great Ouse river. She sat in the car, and could see Mark in the distance making his way toward her. He had not seen her. She took a little bit of time out to think about what she was doing.

They were booked into the Cross Keys Hotel for the night. She knew he had booked a double room. She agreed with herself that she loved Mark, and maybe this would only be a shortlived affair. Part of her was happy and elated, and part of her was sad. She did not know what the future held. After a short while she decided to throw caution to the wind. Why should she not be happy? She was not happy with Gary.

She got out of the car just as Mark approached her from the other side of the car park. He held out his arms and so naturally she walked into them. He kissed her and they started walking through the park. It was a beautiful spot, with little streams branching off the Great Ouse. Each little stream had a wooden curved bridge spanning it, and everywhere were clusters of ducks. They decided to call this place Babylon after the popular song . . . 'By the Rivers of Babylon' sung by Boney M. They talked non stop as they walked, with their arms linked. It was a lovely sunny day, and so peaceful. Margaret felt she had been transported to paradise.

Two hours later they made their way back to the car park and collected their overnight bags and headed for the hotel. It was a very quaint old building standing on one side of the square.

Mark booked them in and they made their way upstairs. It was agreed they would get changed and have dinner. Margaret had brought a new dress which she had bought in Chelmsford in her lunch hour the day before. It had cost a small fortune, but as soon as she had tried it on knew it suited her and she just had to buy it.

It was very simple and fitted her figure well. it was a beautiful shade of pale lilac with a tight bodice and a flared floaty skirt. She took herself off to the bathroom along the corridor from their room and stepped into a lovely hot bath, before changing into her finery. When she returned to their room, Mark took himself off to the bathroom for a shower and by seven o'clock they were on their way downstairs to the restaurant.

Margaret could never remember what she ate, she was mesmerised and fully occupied with Mark. He related to her the people he was working with at Lincoln and the patients they were dealing with. Margaret told him about her visit to Witham and about the little girl who would not eat, and that she was being assigned to the premature baby ward for a few days the following week. Mark kept holding her hand and after finishing off the bottle of wine he had ordered, they returned to their room upstairs.

Margaret was nervous, she had never slept with anyone other than Gary. Mark however made it easy, by slipping out of the room for a while, while she got undressed. When Mark returned he had changed into his dressing gown. He came over to the bed and very gently took her in his arms. 'Maggie I do love you so. I do want you to know that I do not want this to be a short affair, we get on so well together, I am sure we can work something out.' He lifted her chin and bent and kissed her so gently, so passionately, and taking his time he gently made love to her and brought her to the heights. Never had she experienced such wonderful feelings, and she knew those feelings were mutual.

Mark understood her and her needs, and they made love three times before they fell asleep locked in each other's arms.

When she woke the following morning, tears of happiness stung her eyes. *How could this happiness be right?* She thought. But she was in no doubt that she loved Mark. She looked over at Mark who was still asleep. She put her arm over him and smiled. Suddenly he opened his eyes and looked up at her and smiled, 'Good morning my lovely,' he said, then pulled her down next to him where they stayed locked together. They could hear people moving about in the corridor, and regretfully, some time later, decided to get up and dress, before going down to breakfast. They were the last people to eat, it was nearly 10 o'clock, when the breakfast session closed.

They ate a huge English breakfast, before leaving the hotel and heading toward the car park. She dreaded saying goodbye, but again Mark made it easy by saying, 'We must meet up here again next week if that is all right with you?' Her heart lurched 'Fine Mark, about the same time?' she asked. He nodded. He lifted her bag into the boot of her car, and turned, wrapped his arms around her and kissed her again and again. She was breathless. She got into her car and started up the engine. It was now back to St John's Hospital to do some work. As she drove away, he waved and she waved back. What a memorable time they had. She was floating on air.

She soon came down to earth on arrival at the hospital.

She was told that her husband had been at the hospital the evening before and was looking for her, and he had Katy with him. She wondered what was wrong. He was nowhere in the hospital, and the social work secretary said he had left very early that morning, but had left her a message that he was making his way back home as she was not around and would see her at the weekend.

Margaret was panic struck. What on earth did Gary want? He would have to come the evening she was not there. She rang Brenda and told her the situation. Brenda laughed and said, 'Sweetie you were up in Ipswich with me weren't you? We played a game of squash and it got late and you stayed with me for the night.' Ever practical. God Bless Brenda.

Her supervisor asked to see her and asked where she had been. She felt like telling her to mind her own business, but thought better of it. She gave her Brenda's story and it worked.

'Well I would be grateful if you would inform the hospital office if you are to be away, firstly there is the matter of security as well as fire precautions. If there had been a fire in the hospital while you were away, we would have assumed you were still in your room,' she said. 'The other thing is, your husband came up to the hospital to see you, but when you could not be located he had insisted on seeing your room. The staff were most concerned about his behaviour, I suggest you have a word with him. We made no arrangement for him to visit, and if he intends to come again whilst you are still on placement, please ask him to contact you first about it.' The woman stormed out of the office. Margaret felt very deflated. Gary was certainly making things difficult for her, and it could affect her results.

She was not looking forward to going home at the weekend.

******

Later that morning she received a telephone call from Mark. 'Hi beautiful, I miss you,' he said. She smiled into the phone. The memory of their lovemaking presented itself to her. For a moment all other thoughts left her.

Margaret told him about Gary visiting the hospital and how worried she was. She told him about her conversation with Brenda.

'I am so grateful to Brenda, but it means the cat is out of the bag with her,' she told him. She could hear his concern as he pointed out to her that as far as the hospital was concerned, they only cared whether she was in the building or not. Gary however was a different matter.

'I do hope everything will be all right when you go home at the weekend,' he said. 'Call me at my home if there is a problem. I will be back home by 7 o'clock on Friday evening.

Maggie take care, I hope everything is all right. I do love you, and I hope I have not in any way made things awkward for you,' he went on.

'I love you too Mark, I am sure it will be okay, but I cannot think why Gary came up to the hospital. I think he must have been spying on me,' she told him.

'Well we must be very careful in the future,' he concluded. 'Now drive home safely, you are driving this weekend aren't you?' he asked.

'Yes, Jenny is bringing the other three to St John's for 4pm on Friday afternoon,' she explained. 'We should be home by 7 o'clock.' Mark rang off confirming she could ring him, if not he would contact her on Monday morning.

Margaret rang home and spoke to Gary. 'what made you come up to the hospital?' she asked.

'I thought it would be a nice surprise for you, and Katy was missing you,' he told her. 'Where were you? I thought you were at the nurse's home every evening?' he continued to ask.

'Well Brenda asked me up to Ipswich for a game of squash, and to have dinner together, so as I was lonely I agreed to go. I would not have gone, had you told me you were coming to see me,' she replied.

Well at least it was nothing disastrous she thought as she put the phone down.

As she was driving the group towards Hampshire she soon realised that they all knew about last Wednesday. Brenda had told Jenny. Jenny was very prim and proper and frowned on the escapade. Patrick thought it was good fun. But they all stood by her and told no one else.

The weekend flew by. Gary had to work most of the weekend, and Katy never left her side. She hated leaving the child, but told her it would not be long before the course ended, then she would be home with her. Katy clung onto this piece of information.

When she returned to the hospital, she received a telephone call from Mark, in fact he seemed to ring every morning. She was usually checking files she was working on, or making up her notes each morning in her little office. She was always alone, and she loved receiving a call from Mark, it set her up for the day. She confirmed she could get away on Wednesday and would meet him about 4pm at the same place.

On the second week Mark told her he had forgotten to book a room until that morning, but the hotel had been able to find one for them. They made their way upstairs at 6 o'clock to find their room had three single beds in it, all different heights. They looked at each other and laughed.

'So which one shall we sleep in?' he asked her.

'Let us try them all,' she replied.

So they did. The tallest bed was rather hard, and the middle height one was a little narrow, so they tried the little bed which although only three foot wide, seemed the best.

'I think we should call this the three bears room,' she said, and over the next few weeks they had many a laugh about that room when they passed it. Mark always ensured after that that he booked a room well in advance.

On her return to the hospital she learnt that Michael Penn her tutor was coming to see her on Friday morning, for a tutorial session. When he arrived she took him up to her little office and made him a cup of tea. She told him about the cases she had been working on and her current involvement in the premature baby unit. There were two very tiny babies in the unit at present weighing less than two pounds in weight.

He seemed most impressed with her notes and although her supervisor had torn her off a strip about leaving the hospital the week before, had given her good marks. Michael told her that the college was arranging a formal dinner dance during the last week of the course for the whole class. It was to be held at a hotel in Woodbridge. Long dresses were in order.

Except for her black one, she had no need for long dresses, and decided she would make herself one. She was already spending time with the bridal dresses. They were all cut out and ready to sew, but she wanted to have a really nice dress for the dinner dance. She decided that early next week she would go into Chelmsford town centre and purchase some material. It would give her something to do on the evenings she was at the hospital on her own.

During her third week Mark decided to come to Chelmsford on the Wednesday and take her on the train to London to see a show. So on Wednesday they went to see No Sex Please, We Are British. It was terribly funny. They really enjoyed it. They both loved humorous plays, and this was the first of many. They stayed the night in a local guest house just outside Chelmsford.

She told Mark that the following weekend he would be able to watch her on the television. That the evening service was being screened by the BBC for Sunday Half Hour. She also told him that the following Tuesday she would be going to visit the St Charles Treatment Centre at Brentwood where Mary Bell was placed. It was a mental health treatment centre for disturbed people.

He said, 'You lucky thing, it sounds interesting.' She knew he was studying mental health and she would have liked it if he could go as well, but unfortunately that could not happen. What with a visit Jenny had arranged for her at The Turner Village, her last week was very full.

She had to dash home on her last week before leaving St John's because Sarah was playing in a concert on the Saturday. She had her dress to stitch, and also the wedding dresses needed to have a fitting. She was so busy. She had a surprise telephone call from Mark on the Saturday morning, saying he just had to talk with her, he needed to hear her voice. The call lifted her spirits and she waded through her commitments.

'How would you like to come to Lincoln next Wednesday?' he asked her. 'I will find us somewhere to stay, and you can come and see where I am currently working. We can also visit Lincoln Cathedral.'

'It sounds great and will make a change for me to do the long drive, yes, that will be fine,' she told him. He agreed to send her a little map of how to get there. He told her he was so looking forward to seeing her. How she loved him. What would happen the following week, she wondered, for they would be back at the lodgings with Miss Jarvis.

She looked forward to the visit to Lincoln, and on her return to Chelmsford after the weekend she packed all her things together ready for her departure from the hospital the following Friday.

CHAPTER 31

On Wednesday the 24th May Margaret set out for Lincoln. She was in fine spirits. Mark had sent her a drawing of how to get to Lincoln. Firstly she drove up the A1 and turn turned on the A46 which went directly into Lincoln. She then took out his local drawing and the site of the hospital he was at.

She arrived at the hospital about 4pm and parked her car next to his little red peril. They had nicknamed his car weeks ago. It was a red Opel car, but quite small. Mark usually drove when they were together, so she was quite familiar with his car.

He came out to meet her from his office. He told her he had finished for the day. She left her car outside his office and went in his car. As soon as they were outside the hospital he stopped the car and took her in his arms. 'Hi beautiful,' he said. 'Welcome to Lincoln.' She blushed.

He drove her into the city and very soon they were outside the Balmoral Hotel. 'We will be staying here tonight,' he said. 'What do you think?'

The hotel looked very grand, and when they went to their room she saw that they had a beautiful view of Lincoln Cathedral from their window. No sooner were they in their room than they were undressed and in bed. It was so good to feel so close to Mark, she had missed him, and needed him to comfort her. They rose early evening, showered and dressed for dinner. The meal was excellent, and then they strolled through the town centre. There were lots of little shops and as they climbed toward the Cathedral they had a magnificent view of the city.

The following morning they visited the magnificent cathedral straight after breakfast. She admired the beautiful stained glass windows and revelled in the history on the walls and tombs. It felt magical. She was glad she had come, she would not have missed it for the world.

All too soon it was time to return to Chelmsford. Late that afternoon, she made up all her notes concerning the patients she had worked with and handed them to her supervisor before sitting down and finishing the dress she was making for the dinner dance. It was beautiful. There were three layers. Two of taffeta and one of nylon and chiffon in pale cream decorated with tiny sprigs of flowers. The tight bodice suited her slim figure, as well as the beautiful flouncy skirt, which ended at her ankles. She had edged both the cape sleeves and the dress hem with brown velvet ribbon. It was beautiful. As soon as she had completed it she hung it up in a polythene dress bag. She would have to take it home with her the following day and hang it up until she returned in four weeks time for the dinner dance. At least it was finished and she was proud of it.

The four friends returned home for the Whit holiday. Ten days till she returned to Ipswich. She missed Mark, but he continued to telephone her every day, and making sure she was all right.

With her placement ended and all the essays complete, she knew that there would be some free days before the examiners arrived at the college to judge their essays and coursework, as well as their tutors comments. She feared the result.

She returned to Ipswich, and made her way to Sycamore Avenue. As she put her key in the door, Fifi yapped and came to greet her. She had missed the little dog. Fifi jumped up at Margaret and was rewarded with lots of strokes and fuss.

Miss Jarvis was also pleased to see Margaret. She had missed her. Margaret made her way up to her room, and unpacked her bags. A little later she heard Mark arrive.

He knocked on her door. She invited him in, and within minutes she was in his arms and he was kissing her.

'Be careful Mark, Miss Jarvis may come up the stairs and see us,' she implored.

'Blow Miss Jarvis, I have missed you so much, I cannot bear to be apart from you for ten days at a time, it is too much.'

'Maggie come for a walk with me, I want to talk to you,' he said.

She picked up her cardigan and they both left the house. They walked along arm in arm. 'Maggie, it is not practical for us to stay with Miss Jarvis, how do you feel if I find us somewhere to stay at Felixstowe until we finish the course?' he asked.

'I think that would be grand,' she replied.

'I believe there is a hotel along the front called Wessex Hotel, where I am sure we would be comfortable,' he went on.

'It is fine by me,' she replied.

So the following day they gave their notices to Miss Jarvis who looked most disappointed, but thanked them both for being such good tenants.

On the Friday Margaret loaded her car with her typewriter and her rug, and the teasmade and her spare clothes, and took them all home. There was very little room for the other three car occupants' luggage, but everything was squeezed in.

The following Monday she returned and dropped off her friends where they were each staying, and then met Mark in the college car park. She parked her car and locked it. Picked up her bag and climbed into his car. They drove off to Felixstowe.

The Wessex Hotel was very nice, and they both enjoyed the privacy it afforded them, and also allowed them to be together. They made love every night that week, and drove each day to the college, where they tried hard to conceal their happiness from the other class members.

The last week of the course loomed ahead. The examiners were in the college for three days, and on the third day everyone was biting their fingernails, and were so stressed out. On the Wednesday they were given their results. Two members on the course were referred and had to do further work over the next few weeks, but seventeen of them had passed including Mark and herself. Everyone was jubilant. That evening everyone went to the local pub for a celebratory drink. They were all going to attend the dinner dance which had been arranged at Melton Grange the following evening.

Mark had brought his grey pinstriped suit for the dance and she had brought the dress she had made.

On Thursday evening after a quick bath Margaret put on the dress, and pinned up her hair. She looked stunning. She was just completing her make up in the mirror, when Mark asked her to close her eyes, She felt him place something around her neck. When she opened her eyes she saw a beautiful St Christopher pendant on a silver chain. She turned, flung her arms around his neck and thanked him.

She put the stole she had brought with her around her shoulders, and they set off for the hotel in his car.

When they arrived at Melton Grange, all their colleagues were there. He took her arm, and she heard whisperings, but took no notice. It was a fantastic party, the food was excellent and the music flowed all evening.

Mark danced with her, and never appeared to leave her side. They stood and talked with Jenny and Brenda, and Sean and Dorothy, and the waiters handed them glasses of wine and champagne. Suddenly the music changed and their song was being played.

The Rivers of Babylon - she pulled Mark onto the floor, not caring what people were thinking, and danced until the music ended. Then he kissed her. There was a babble of voices, but they took no notice.

It was past midnight when they returned to their hotel. Unfortunately they found the front door locked. They had forgotten to tell the reception that they would be late back. They rang the bell but nothing happened. After the third time of ringing the bell someone came and let them in.

They apologised, but giggled all the way up to their room.

They hung up their finery, and climbed into bed. It suddenly hit them that the following day they were returning home, Margaret to Hampshire and Mark to Yorkshire. They would be miles apart. They clung to each other, and tried hard to obliterate their morbid thoughts. All too soon dawn broke, and with it a nasty wet rainy day.

When they climbed out of bed, their hearts were heavy and sad. They dressed and packed their bags, and went downstairs for breakfast. Margaret did not feel much like eating, and Mark only had coffee. She had agreed to go with him into Ipswich and choose some classical records for him to take back to Yorkshire. They drove into town and made their way to WH Smiths, and purchased six records which she chose. It was time to leave. They drove to the college and put her luggage into her car boot. They sat in Mark's car, there seemed nothing to say. He held out his arms to her and she melted against him, suddenly the tears rolled down her cheeks, and she started to sob. She did not want to go home. When she finally looked up at Mark she found he was crying too. They held each other for what seemed an eternity.

Eventually Mark said they must get started, it was getting late. 'Maggie I know it is going to be hard, but you must be brave. You have to go on holiday in a few days with your family to Spain and I have to go on holiday with my family to Malta. The holidays are booked. We have commitments,' he said, knowing full well his heart was breaking.

'As soon as we are back we will arrange to meet regularly that I promise, but we must go home now.' He felt a heel. He did not want to leave her either, but he knew they had things to resolve. Margaret nodded, and opened the car door, and climbed into her car. She felt numb, having dried her eyes she was resolute she would try hard not to cry again.

She switched on her engine, it roared into life. With a great deal of willpower she put the car in gear, smiled at Mark and waved to him. He waved back and watched her drive out of the college car park.

She drove toward the A12 and the long journey home. A few miles down the road she pulled into a lay by and wiped the tears from her eyes, she could hardly see the road. She sat for some while until she felt calmer, and tried to think of her family at home, and eventually she once more put the big car into gear and drove non stop to Hampshire.

At least she was a qualified social worker now. She was however dreading the holiday to Salou in Spain. It had been booked months ago. It had been decided she would want a holiday after the course ended. This was probably right, but her heart was heavy. Gary was coming with her, as well as Katy, Sarah and her boyfriend Jack. She had three days at home before they departed. She was kept busy washing clothes and packing clothes, and acquiring toiletries to take with them. Everyone seemed excited. She kept wondering what Mark was doing.

The day before the family flew to Spain she had a telephone call from Mark. It was so good to hear from him. He told her he was not looking forward to going to Malta with his wife, his sister and her husband even though it was only a week. She knew how he felt. She told him how much she missed him, and he commiserated with her and hoped she had a good flight, and promised to telephone her as soon as she returned. He reminded that he loved her dearly, and he was positive things would sort themselves out, although it may take a while.

'Love you,' she said.

'Love you too,' he replied.

******

So the family set out to Gatwick and had a reasonably good flight to Spain, The hotel at Salou was rather mediocre, but the room problem loomed large as soon as they arrived. They had three single rooms allocated to them and one double room. One for each of the children and the double one for Gary and herself. Oh Lord she had forgotten she was having to share a room with him, notwithstanding their room was right over the nightclub and the noise on the first evening was horrendous.

Margaret went to see if they could change rooms. Unfortunately they did not have any other single rooms, but did manage to change their double room to the other side of the building. It was good, in as much as they were nearer to the children's rooms.

When she was getting undressed Gary came over to her, and put his arms around her and said, 'Come on

Margaret, let us let bygones be bygones, let us make a fresh start.' He went on, 'All that college work has finished, and we can start to enjoy life.'

Margaret froze, 'I do not want to start again Gary. I have had years of trying to improve our lives and our relationship, but it is over, is that clear?' she glared at him. 'Do not come near me, do you understand? I have only come on this holiday because it was booked. Just try to make the best of it like I will, for the sake of the children.' She stood her ground.

Gary shrugged, leered at her and said, 'You will change your mind before long.' She knew better.

They went onto the beach each day, it was very hot and Gary only believed in rolling up his trouser legs to the knee and rolling up his shirt to the elbows. He did not like undressing on the beach. The girls loved the sand and also paddling in the sea. They became embroiled in the hotel activities, and Margaret made the best of it all.

The day they were to leave for home, they packed their cases as they had to be out of their rooms by midday. They put their suitcases into a room in the lobby of the hotel and went to have lunch. The waiter brought their plates with roast chicken and vegetables. Everyone seemed to enjoy it. It tasted all right, but within half an hour of leaving the restaurant Margaret was violently sick, shortly after feeling ill she also had diarrhoea. She had no room to go to, but the reception staff found her an empty room where she could lay down. She did not feel like laying down, she spent all her time in the bathroom being sick. Gary went off and asked for the hotel doctor. He could see she was most unwell.

When the doctor came he told her she had some sort of salmonella poisoning, and gave her horrid liquid to drink.

It made her feel worse. The doctor said she would have to go to the hospital.

'No I am not going. I am going on the plane back to England,' she shouted at him.

'I am sorry, I cannot allow you to fly, you are too ill Madam,' the doctor went on.

She glared at him from the floor of the bathroom. 'I am going on the aeroplane with my family later today, and that is final,' she was once more sick.

A few hours later her symptoms abated, although she felt terribly ill. By the time the coach arrived to take them all to the airport at seven o'clock, she was worn out but very determined she was going to make it home. They let her lay along the back seat, and she tried to sleep. The coach journey would last an hour. At the airport she sat most distraught on a chair. She soon learned that the flight was delayed and they would not take off until 4am at the earliest.

It was most uncomfortable on the chair but better than the
Cold hard floor. Eventually they boarded their flight. She was frightened to drink anything even though she was thirsty. She did not want to be sick again.

She fell asleep on the plane, and could not face any food being put in front of her. When they landed it was half past six. By the time they had been through passport control and collected their luggage from the carousel it was past eight o'clock.

She left the family group and headed for the ladies toilets. She looked in the mirror and hardly recognised herself. She looked so pale, and her hair looked a mess. She had a wash and brushed her hair, then decided she had to ring Mark.

She slipped out of the toilets and found a telephone kiosk. She looked up his home number in her diary and dialled it. He answered straightaway. He had arrived home from Malta two days before.

'Oh Mark, I have had an awful time,' she told him, and went on to explain all about the holiday, culminating in how she was at present. He was aghast, and commiserated with her. 'Maggie, I love you kiddo, get home and I will ring you later, I'll organise something, keep your chin up.'

She felt better for talking to him. Everyone piled into Gary's car which had been parked near the airport, and within an hour they were back in Harmsworth.

Sarah cooked a meal, though Maggie was still not eating anything, but had started drinking sips of water. She emptied the cases and put the dirty clothes into the washing machine. Jack went off back to his family home after dinner, and Katy followed Margaret around. The child was really worried about her mother.

That evening Gary took himself off, she knew not where, and did not care. At eight o'clock the telephone rang. It was Mark.

'Maggie, how are you?' he asked her. She told him she was feeling a lot better, but was very tired.

'How would you like to meet me in St Neots in two days time?' he asked her. Her heart raced. 'I would love to,' she replied, 'but I would have to make some arrangements first.'

'Fine, give me a ring tomorrow. I will be in my office all morning. I love you Maggie, never forget that.' She loved the sound of his voice.

'I know, I love you too, I'll ring you tomorrow morning,' she rang off.

The following morning early she drove to see Joan Beak and asked for her help. She readily agreed to take Katy to school and collect her, as well as cooking the dinner for

Gary and the two girls. She would do the same on Thursday, and it was agreed Margaret would be back around 6pm.

She rang Mark and told him, and arranged a time for the following day. She was feeling better and had eaten a boiled egg for breakfast. She went down to see Sam Jackson at the Area Office. He told her she need not return to work for another two weeks, especially after he heard about her illness in Spain.

She decided she would go and see a solicitor during those two weeks and try and organise a divorce from Gary. She could not live with him anymore, of that she was sure.

So on Wednesday 12th July she drove to St Neots. She had the wireless on in her car, and she felt happy. Very soon she would be with Mark. She knew Mark loved her unconditionally, she could be herself with him.

She pulled into the car park, and there he was standing next to the little red peril. He smiled at her, and she smiled back. She parked the car, and got out, turned round and ran into his arms. He held her so tight she could hardly breathe, but she knew this is where she belonged. She loved him and he loved her. He was her soul mate and she could not imagine life without him. They would work things out she was sure.

About the Author

Jean Reddy was born in London in 1936 and lived through the Blitz as a small child, before being evacuated to North Wales in 1942 for three years.

Her early life provides the background she vividly created for her first novel 'The Evacuee Girl'.

Her new book 'CHALLENGES' reflects her very controversial life and the emotional turmoil she lived through.

This sequel is a continuation of the story of her life from the time she left school in 1951, through her attempts to find happiness while striving towards her ambition to become a Welfare Officer. Her life focuses on the ups and downs of married life, and her need to fulfill her dreams.

She now lives happily in North Hampshire wth her second husband Harry, surrounded by her large family of children and grandchildren, who all live within a fifteen mile radius.